African Delights

African Delights

Siphiwo Mahala

The publication of this book would not have
been possible without the assistance of the
Jacana Literary Foundation (JLF).

JLF JACANA LITERARY FOUNDATION

The Jacana Literary Foundation is dedicated to the
advancement of writing and reading in South Africa, and
is supported by the Multi-Agency Grants Initiative (MAGI)
through whose generous funding the JLF aims to nurture South
African literature and bibliodiversity.

First published by Jacana Media (Pty) Ltd in 2011

10 Orange Street
Sunnyside
Auckland Park 2092
South Africa
+2711 628 3200
www.jacana.co.za

© Siphiwo Mahala, 2011

ISBN 978-1-4314-0251-9
Job No. 001577
Set in Cochin 10.5/14pt

Edited by Helen Moffett
Cover design by Maggie Davey and Shawn Paikin
Cover image by James Mathibeng
Printed and bound by Ultra Litho (Pty) Limited, Johannesburg

See a complete list of Jacana titles at www.jacana.co.za

Contents

◆

Foreword

Mandla Langa

◆

To MAKE SENSE OF and to claim for our own Siphiwo Mahala's collection of short stories, a smorgasbord of tasty titbits aptly named *African Delights*, we first need to understand why Mahala felt compelled to draw us into his imagined universe. It is a universe eloquently evoked by the Uruguayan writer, Eduardo Galeano, in his essay "In Defence of the Word", which appears in his *Days and Nights of Love and War*.

> One writes out of a need to communicate and to commune with others, to denounce that which gives pain and to share that which gives happiness. One writes against one's solitude and against the solitude of others... One writes for the people whose luck or misfortune one identifies with – the hungry, the sleepless, the rebels and the wretched of the earth – and the majority of them are illiterate.

The notion of writing for the illiterate is probably self-contradictory, since it raises the question of access to the written symbols that encode words. Illiteracy, also, is a darkness to which a vast majority of our people has been subjected. During a visit to Beijing in 1998, this writer was briefly separated from his group in Tiananmen Square. Panicked, he couldn't tell where he was or how to get to his hotel; all the signage was in Chinese characters, and he didn't know the language. An illiterate person in South Africa is that and more; his or her bewilderment is compounded by the stigma that attaches itself to the unlettered, who are usually dismissed as ignorant and uncivilised.

But, to write for the constituency of the downtrodden – the wretched of the earth – can only be achieved through a complete identification with the plight of people whom the African-American poet Margaret Walker calls "all the people/ all the faces/ all the Adams and Eves and their countless generations". This cannot be done, cannot be achieved if the writer fails to master the language that strikes a chord with his or her readers.

The readers, in a country like South Africa, might not necessarily need to know the alphabet; but they must be gifted with the patience to listen to a story being read out. As a form, the short story lends itself to being read out and uses fewer formal elements than the novel. For instance, it does not face the hurdles of developing those major elements of fiction: character, plot, theme, point of view, and so on.

Not too long ago, the South African media, especially Radio 702, championed the cause of the short story. This was in line with worldwide developments, notably in the United Kingdom, where the National Short Story Week boosted the celebration of the short story. The initiative is an annual awareness event that directs the public and the media to the short story and short story writers, publishers and events. According to publicity material posted on its website, the NSSW "is intended as a framework for promoting literary events and publications at a national and local level".

Elsewhere, for instance, within the South African Department of Arts and Culture – which is where Siphiwo

Mahala currently works – there has been a flurry of activity to bolster interest around books, reading and publishing. For instance, from 5 to 10 September 2011, the South African Book Development Council and the DAC co-hosted this country's National Book Week.

Even in the age of electronic publishing, postings, blogging and gadgetry, there is still something about people converging around words and their physical manifestation in books and journals. Even though society is being programmed or enjoined, whether by economic or social imperatives to enjoy solitary entertainment, nothing takes the place of throngs huddled around the latest literary offering, possibly by a young author, to marvel and encourage (or, in cases of talents bypassed by fame and fortune, to feed the green monster).

It is a moot point that talent eludes the majority of any society and chooses a select minority. It is also axiomatic that talent waxes brightest in instances where its possessor strives for excellence. A country might have a huge population with diverse experiences; that fact alone does not necessarily translate into creative output any more than the number of aspirant soccer players in any one country produces an equivalent of, say, Brazil or the Cameroun. For many years, Cuba and Hungary led the world in cinema production despite their respective small populations. It all resulted from the national character, the political will of the leaders, and the cultural policies of those countries. What this means, simply, for the purposes of this foreword, is that a people might have a wonderful store of historical experiences, the stuff of which stories are made, but somehow fail to share those stories with the rest of humanity. Their collective life experiences become akin to Thomas Gray's flower, born to blush unseen.

And that is a tragedy because, from Aesop's fables,

izinganekwane or *üntsomi* that heightened our grasp of humankind's complex nature, tales, myths and legends of Native American Indians or the Ijaw in Nigeria to scriptures and songs, these narratives entertained societies while giving them lessons of life. Who can forget the tales of animals, which were our weekly entertainment, at a time of this country's ignorance, when radio was a vehicle to broadcast poisonous state propaganda and television a dreaded instrument of the devil?

For many years, the stories of this country – as well as the stories from this country – were told in the same vein as hunting stories told by hunters. There was censorship, which proscribed any narrative that sought to invest the majority of this country, black people, with human qualities. This meant that, for the sake of survival and for an unconscionable length of time, black people had to collude in a lie about their unsuitability as members of the human race; even more so, white people were also lied to and grew up with a sense of superiority that was at odds with reality. Everyone, therefore, the hunter and the lion, was infantilised by the policies of an uninformed cabal.

There have been attempts by black writers – and if truth be told, by some white writers – to tell the South African story. And here, people will differ on what constitutes that story, seeing that there have been narratives that come out of this country that have absolutely nothing to do with the heartbeat of this troubled country and its troubled people. Black people, too, have written stories about South Africa – a South Africa that exists, possibly, in those waxworks studios where reasonable facsimiles of the human body are manufactured. The form is there, but the soul is absent. This is where artists create good-looking corpses.

The succession of literary movements largely mirrored the political radicalisation of the downtrodden. There is a trajectory that traces forms of expression from the supplications of the British colonial administration of the 1900s, which saw the rise of talents such as Sol T Plaatje; the so-called *Drum* school of writing reflected, partly, the hardening of attitudes following mass removals, Sharpeville and the armed struggle; the Black Consciousness movement – itself having the Black Power movement in the United States as a creative crucible – in the 1970s. The literature of the 1980s up till the dawn of liberation, especially poetry, was an exhortation to action.

Siphiwo Mahala is clearly influenced by none other than Can Themba, who was the most brilliant chronicler of the anxieties of the time covered by the *Drum* writers. There were others, Eskia Mphahlele, Bloke Modisane, Lewis Nkosi, Arthur Maimane, Nat Nakasa, to name a few, who were the bright lights of the period. It was Can Themba, perhaps, who most personified what he wrote: he lived fast, drank hard and died relatively young, although he didn't quite pull off the trick of maintaining a good-looking corpse, *a la* Willard Motley's mordant dictum.

Now that we've cleared the undergrowth – to borrow a phrase from a Constitutional Court judge – let's get back to business.

Mahala's *African Delights* is a timely intervention in our literary life. The book, consisting of twelve short stories grouped in threes, explores the whole gamut of modern South African life. Most of the stories are told in the first person, with the ones using the third-person point of view tending to be longer, including the title story.

Even though Mahala tackles important themes that relate to human development, triumphs and tears, he maintains a distance that allows him to deploy humour with devastating effect. The laughter is not at the expense of his characters; he explores rather than exploits the frailties of his protagonists. He laughs with rather than at his characters.

This indulgent attitude to the weaknesses of his characters – who are themselves victims of stronger external forces – disappears completely when he turns his sharp wit to the adventures of that class of human colloquially called the tenderpreneur. These are the beneficiaries of black economic empowerment tenders, who've not raised any capital, but who are conspicuous consumers. They possess cars the size of battleships and other accoutrements, such as young trophy wives who, in turn, rob them blind both in and out of the marital bed.

Mahala reflects the bewilderment of this class without mercy.

Contemporary South Africa, a state in flux, needs to read these stories to understand how it is seen by some of the sharpest commentators that this democracy has produced. Millions of rands are wasted on focus groups that strive to produce a blueprint, a roadmap, towards a livable future for this country and its people. The pony-tailed consultants need look no further because we have in our midst prophets who give us a glimpse into what we are. And, more chillingly, what we're destined to become.

Eduardo Galeano might have been reading Mahala's book, reading between the lines, hearing what has been left unexpressed. He wrote:

> In these lands of young people … the tick-tock of the time bomb obliges those who rule to sleep with one eye open.

I am part of the fellowship of writers that welcomes the addition of *African Delights* to the body of South African arts and letters.

PART ONE

The Suit Stories
A tribute to Can Themba

The Suit Continued

◆

IT IS ANNOYING WHEN people keep telling the story of a woman who was tormented by her husband because I left my suit in his house. You know, people think that she was the only one who suffered. But then, I don't really blame them because maybe that's how Can Themba wanted them to feel.

The only thing he mentions in his propaganda piece, *The Suit*, is that I ran away. Did he think that that was the end of the story for me? Did he think that I, a respected schoolteacher, enjoyed running around the streets of Sophiatown in my underwear? Did he think that I felt no remorse when the woman decided to put an end to her life? No, those things could not just happen and leave me feeling no shame. Besides, I had my own humiliation to deal with. I'm neither a writer nor a journalist as Can Themba was, but I thought I should jot down a few lines so people know my side of the story before I sink six feet under. This is not a confession, but a testimony.

First of all, it was never my style to have dealings with married women. You see, there is this thing about a woman: if she wants you, she is sure to get you. Unlike us; if we want her, we have to go a long way trying to impress her. Somehow I feel that women do take advantage of us men. In fact, women of those days had a great deal of advantage over us.

When I met this girl, I had had a few tots of brandy, not to get drunk; just to cure my body after a Sunday afternoon of heavy drinking. Please note that I'm addressing her as a "girl" because that's what she looked like when I first met her. She didn't seem like a married woman at all. I know when alcohol registers itself in a man's head, even the ugliest woman suddenly becomes attractive, but this was not the case. She caught my eye with her red mini-dress that girls used to wear in those days. *Ag man*, I forgot that you young people wouldn't know those dresses. Let me just say, they are seductively equivalent to the tight shorts and the skimpy blouses that young girls wear these days. When I see these girls, I feel like getting young again. I may have a bald patch and a wrinkled skin, but my heart feels as young as ever.

But that's not the point. What I'm saying is that this woman took advantage of me the first day we met. It was during lunch break and I went to Thirty-nine Steps, as I usually did on Monday mornings. That's what we used to do with Can when he was teaching at Madibane High School in Western. I had been friends with Can since our university days at Fort Hare. You see, this is what I like about being a teacher: you are within the community and you can always take a moment out to rid yourself of a hangover. We usually bought our hooch from Thirty-nine Steps and took it to Can's "House of Truth". Decent guys in Sophiatown used to drink there.

On this morning my throat was as dry as a desert, and my whole body was shivering. The noise that the children made sounded like a beehive inside my head. Every word I said trying to silence them echoed in my aching head, and they wasted no time in making irritating whispers and pointing towards my direction. Hangover was playing with me, I tell you. I knew the only remedy was to pay a quick visit to Thirty-nine Steps.

Can was now working as a journalist for *Drum*, and I

knew I'd find him there. Well, he was not there yet and I did not mind having a brandy half-jack by myself. Fatty, the enormous shebeen queen, seemed to be pleased that I took the drink on credit. Man, that woman knew how to do business. She was always happier when you went there without money because she would charge you double the amount. You would not think about that until at the end of the month when you had to pay her. As friendly as she was when she gave you the drink, Fatty took no nonsense when she wanted her money. Sometimes I just felt she increased the bill because she knew I was a bit drunk when I initially made the credit. I didn't dare to complain because Fatty was never reluctant to squash a man with her bare hands.

Here I am again dwelling on shebeen life, but that is not what this testimony is about. It is about this woman who got me into trouble. I call her "woman" because I never knew her real name. Yes, I slept with her a couple of times, but still I did not know her name because she called me "sweetie" (it was the first time a woman had taken to calling me that), and I had to refer to her in the same way. I only knew her name after I read Can's story. Matilda (as Can calls her) came in and sat on the arm of the sofa I was sitting on. I knew she was attracted to me because I was looking good. Although I was not a full-time member because I had a decent job, I was often associated with the Americans – that notorious Sophiatown gang. I had on my Humphrey Bogart hat, my blue suit, and brown-and-white Florsheims, "America's finest shoes" (as the advert claimed). Even the *Mapantsulas* of these days wouldn't match my style during those days, let alone a man who wore khaki-green messenger uniforms. I was *mjita van Kofifi*, I tell you.

Matilda was just one of many women who couldn't wait to jump into bed with me. Okay, to make a long story short, Matilda asked why I drank there because it was not the right place for gentlemen like me, especially during school hours. I told her it was the only place where I could drink. She said no, I must come over to her place and finish what's left of the brandy there. Well, needless to mention, drinking was not the first thing we did when we got to her place. In fact, it went down well after we gave each other some bodily pleasures.

There is nothing as nice as something you are stealing. I knew very well that my wife would not have been happy to find me there. But, nonetheless, it was good; I really enjoyed my time with Matilda. It became a habit for me to spend some time during my lunch breaks at Matilda's place. You know, there was this thing about her: she was not a nagging woman. One thing about women when you have an affair is they usually ask you about your other relationships. How many kids have you got? Are you married? Do you like your wife? Things like that. I really hate it because the inquisitiveness forces you to give her ears what they want to hear. It's better when we do what brings us together and leave other business alone. Finish *en klaar*!

Matilda never asked anything other than for me to come back the following day. For that reason, even my wife never suspected a thing until that day you all know about. In fact, it became known because of Can. I only find solace in that he never mentioned my name. It was that old walking radio Maphikela who spread rumours. I must be honest and say I felt a bit of relief when that big-mouthed, woman-like man took his exit from this world. It seemed like the older he got, the longer his tongue grew.

I suspect Can was one of Maphikela's co-conspirators in setting me up. You see, journalists like Can and Henry Nxumalo were real trouble those days. They were willing to risk their lives in their pursuit of a scoop. Actually, that's how Henry died (bless his soul). I particularly liked Henry because he was dedicated to fighting the injustices. As *Mr Drum*, Henry exposed the brutal treatment farm labourers got.

No matter how Africans were divided those days, there was this lingering bond that always brought us together. We were all victims of apartheid. Together we became a potent force that fought against a common enemy. Besides, there was this looming threat, since 1939, that Sophiatown was going to be demolished. Even the Berliners and the Gestapo, who were the worst enemies in the world of gangsterism, attended the same meetings in the name of preserving the only free territory we had inside South Africa. Together we sang one song: *Asiyi ndawo*, we won't move. Our resistance campaigns turned out to be like farting in a deep ocean when heavily armed police came with bulldozers to demolish Sophiatown in 1955. The Sophiatown we loved was destroyed, but many of us carried it in our hearts to exile.

Can was a good writer, but I can't understand why he would exploit his writing skills by telling reality that was not to be told. Even my grandchildren today know about my ordeal. I understand now that Can was not the major herald in delivering the news to Philemon, but he knew that I was going to get caught that day. You see, I was smoking my Lexington while Matilda rested her head on my chest like a baby clinging to its mother on a stormy evening.

Suddenly Matilda whispered: "That's him!"

"That's who?" I asked.

"That's my husband."

"A husband. Where, what are you talking about?"

"My husband is here. He's opening the door."

By that time I could hear footsteps coming towards the bedroom. There was no time for asking too many questions. Before I could think of anything, the doorknob turned, and the man was inside the room, wearing his khaki-green uniform. I was there naked in his bed with his wife.

"What should I do?" I thought.

The man headed straight for his wardrobe and I knew he was looking for something dangerous – a gun or a knife. I was not interested in finding out which one because that meant I would be carried out of that house – head first. A black man killing another black man was never taken as a serious offence during those days. People did not fear being arrested because a black man could go to jail for not having a pass anyway. Besides, even the law would not protect a man who had been found in bed with another man's wife. The only thing that came to my mind was that I must get out of that house before he turned from the wardrobe. I swiftly put on my boxer shorts and jumped out the window, holding my vest in my hand. I ran while putting on the vest, oblivious of the people who were watching. Apparently among those people was the Sophiatown herald, Maphikela, with whose courtesy Can received the news. Maphikela must have swallowed a small radio during his early days.

I ran and ran and kept running until I heard someone shouting, "Pace-up, pace-up, *meneer*." It was only at that moment that I thought about looking back to see if anyone was following. There was no one, but I could not stop abruptly because that would have invited suspicion from passers-by. Fortunately, I spotted two young fellows who were jogging. One thing I liked about people those days is that you could just join anyone who was on the road. I joined these guys and as my pace was a bit faster than theirs, they picked up speed. We were now racing each other. After a couple of minutes of running with them, one asked, "What sport do you play?"

"I run." I could not say anything longer as I was already gasping for air.

After a brief pause the other one asked: "Do you normally run on bare feet?"

"Yes," I said in between breaths, "especially when I'm preparing for cross-country." I realised this was not good company to keep, so I took the closest turn that would join Ray Street, which led to Edith Street where my house was. As I entered Edith Street, my legs were giving up, and my house seemed to be moving further away.

Now my worry was that Grace might be home when I got there. Okay, let me just say it was one of the few days that the Lord actually listened and responded well to my prayers. She was not back from work yet. What a relief. I reached for my keys, but couldn't find the pocket. It was only at that moment that it crossed my mind that the house keys were in the suit that I was wearing that day. My house keys, my wallet and my pass were left in the suit. The blue suit, my best suit, my wedding suit, was trapped in another man's house. As I was standing there still searching my vest hoping that the keys might have been stuck somewhere, I felt a tap on my shoulder. The first thing that came to my mind was that the man had been following me, and I was now busted.

"Terence, why do you look so terrified?" said a familiar voice as I turned to look. I'm not sure whether I got relieved or more nervous when I discovered that it was my wife.

"Hey, Grace, it's you. I thought it was these silly boys. You see, they have been saying funny things because I'm dressed like this." I said this because I could see in her eyes that she was concerned about my attire, or should I say, my lack of attire.

"Why are you wearing these things? Where is your suit?"

"No, Grace, you see we were having Funny Day at school and I forgot that we had to leave our suits and wear casual. They took my suit so I would look funny. You know those things like Guy Fawkes Day?"

"So they had to humiliate you and let you go home like this?" she said, surveying me from top to bottom. I had to find someone else to blame.

"Grace, you don't know these principals. Because we are under them, they think that they own us. They said I was being disobedient when I refused to take off my clothes. And you know I have had several warnings already."

"Your warnings are due to your drinking habits, I don't blame them ... and where are your shoes?"

"*Eish*, you won't believe this. They didn't even give me a chance to put them on. Now please open the door because I don't want the whole of Sophiatown to see me like this."

That was indeed the one honest thing I said to her that day. I didn't want any more people to see me looking like that.

I was relieved when she finally opened the door. I felt like remaining indoors forever. My heart was still racing like a dog chasing a rabbit. It was only at that moment that I felt the pain of having run on bare feet through the dusty streets of Sophiatown. My feet were swelling. Blood was oozing from my toes, and I had to wash my feet before Grace noticed. Grace began pumping the primus stove in order to boil water. I filled the washing basin with cold water and washed my feet.

"Terence, are you washing now?" she shouted from the other room. I could hear her clearly in our two-roomed matchbox. There was not too much privacy there. You could hear what your next-door neighbour was doing with his wife at any time.

"Yes, I'm gonna wash with cold water. You can just make tea with that water you boiled." I knew she liked saving so much. She always complained that I spent too much money on drinks.

"All right. Wash up so that we can go fetch your suit then."

"No, Grace, don't be in a hurry. I am a bit tired now. I will go there later."

"If you are embarrassed, I don't mind fetching it myself."

"No, no, don't worry about it. I'll go there myself." She compromised even though I could see in her eyes that she was suspicious. I loved my suit and I was very desperate to have it back, but I could not go to that man's house at that point.

I thought I had survived the storm, but it became clear that it was only the whirlwind. My wife always ironed my suit every day for me to wear. When I woke up the following morning, I only found my vest and boxer shorts nicely ironed and waiting for me.

"Where is the suit that I am supposed to wear today, Grace?"

"Your suit is at school, Terry. Didn't you say you left it there? You can just go and get dressed there."

"But I can't go to school like this."

"But you came from school like that."

"Grace, it's different, yesterday was Funny Day. Today isn't."

"I guess that's what you'll have to tell your principal, Terry. You are not putting on another suit until you bring that one."

I knew Grace when she was determined to do something.

There was no way she would change her mind. I suspected somebody had already told her what had happened the previous day. I could not go to school without a suit on. My suit, my pass, my shoes and my house keys were in another man's house; the man whose wife I had been sleeping with for the previous three months. I had to find a way of confessing to my wife.

I cleared my throat and called her. "Grace..." I instinctively placed my hand on my forehead and looked down. My eyes darted from her face to the floor, back to her face and then to the ceiling. She knew from my mannerisms I was about to tell some twisted truth.

"My suit is not really left at school. You see, what happened yesterday..."

I noticed a frown on her face and I knew that she would not take too kindly to what I was about to say.

"Actually, the principal gave it to this boy and he is keeping it in his home."

"Do you know the house?"

"No, yes I do, but you see I have to get dressed first. I can't go there like this. You don't want your husband to walk around the streets of Sophiatown in underwear, do you?"

"In fact, I don't mind, especially when he decides to give his clothes to some *boy* that I don't know. You are not going to wear another suit until you come back with that one."

Well, I never believed in arguing with a woman. She's my woman; I had to find a way of twisting her mind. A man is not a man until he knows how to get himself out of trouble at the worst of times.

"All right, let me go like this, then." I left the house in the same attire as the previous day. I went straight to my brother's house, which was just two blocks from mine. I was a bit taller than my brother. I wore his suit even though his pants held my thighs so tight that I could barely stretch my legs. The arms of the jacket ended just half way down my arms. Since he always wore his only pair of Jarman shoes, I wore his tennis shoes, waterlogged from a heavy downpour the last time they were worn. Cakes of mud had dried on them, changing their original white colour into something brownish. Needless to mention, they were a size or two smaller than mine, and as I walked each step felt like a sharp needle piercing my toes.

School children derived their pleasures from my attire in those few days. Every time I turned to write something on the board they would begin to giggle, and I knew what was so exciting to them. I never smiled, even at the funniest joke, and I used the rod at the slightest offence.

When lunch break finally arrived, I didn't even think that Matilda's husband might be home. I just wanted to get my suit and end whatever had brought us together. When I got there, Matilda told me about her husband's hospitality. They were serving my suit supper and treating it like an important visitor. For that reason, I could not take my suit because Philemon valued it so much that he would kill Matilda if she did not take good care of it – "good care" meaning that it had to be fed and kept within the family.

I could not believe how cruel that man was. Perhaps he was as cruel as my wife was to me. I had to spend three weeks wearing my brother's clothes and dropping them off after school, as my brother had to wear his suit during his night visits to shebeens or white men's businesses to supplement his monthly income. I had to be very careful about where I walked because not possessing a pass reduced me to a criminal in the eyes of the law. Eventually I had to confess to my wife because I could not stand the humiliation of entering my house half-naked every day.

"Grace, I hear that my suit has been confiscated by a certain man," I began rather casually, trying to hide the guilt that filled my heart.

"What do you mean, confiscated?"

"I mean, the boy's father found the suit there and thought it could belong to his wife's lover. So he is keeping it until the owner reveals himself."

"All right. In that case, I'll be more than pleased to go there with you."

I had no choice but to let Grace go with me when I went to collect my suit. As we walked, my mind danced back and forth: how stupid it was for me to fall into this woman's trap; how inconsiderate of me not to think the woman might be married; how foolish I looked when I walked into my house in underwear.

The sight that confronted us when we got there still haunts me to this day. We found Philemon crying helplessly over Matilda's body. My suit was still sitting on a chair with a plate filled with food in front of it. Instead of going for my suit, I just broke down and cried alongside Philemon. I even forgot about my wife who came with the understanding that we were there to take my suit from a silly schoolboy, whose father had confiscated it due to his jealousy and insecurity.

I was more concerned about Matilda's death. My fear was the indignity of fingers being pointed at me as an adulterer, a killer and a devil who had had the audacity to walk into another man's house and sleep with his wife in his bed. The best thing I can do at this stage is to let people know that I am not as inhuman as Can made people think.

The Dress That
Fed the Suit

Zukiswa Wanner

◆

DEAR PHIL,

By the time you read this letter, I will be dead.

I am not sure how you will feel about my death since
you have been killing me mentally bit by bit ever since
that day many weeks ago when Terry jumped out of our
bedroom window in his underwear. Maybe you will finally
forgive me.

Maybe society will never absolve me of this final act of
wanting to be free, or indeed the infidelity that led to this
suicide, but I felt I owed it to you to explain. Thus this
note.

On that fateful day when my perfect world came
crashing down, I could not believe my eyes. In an instant,
the man who had thought me an angel lost all faith in me,
while the man who pleased and amused me in other ways
was gone, never to return again. When you came in, and I
whispered to Terry, "That's him. My husband," I know he
could not believe it either.

What I do not understand is how Terry could ever have
believed that a beautiful woman like me could be single.
But even more than that, did he think I had my own place,
in this age and era? Where the black man is oppressed, but
the black woman even more so because she cannot own
or rent property? After all, I spent most mornings with

27

him (except during the weekends) and he never saw me taking in any washing, so just where did he think I got my money from? He certainly did not see me running a shebeen or going for a "night shift" at the corner of Victoria Road. Ahhh. To be a simple man. May be he was drunk all through the three months I was with him. But then again, Terry and I never did talk much.

I never wanted you to find out the way you did. If truth be told, I never wanted you to find out full stop. I have my suspicions about how you found out. My mind tells me, even now, as I take my final breaths, that it probably came from that old woman MaMaphikela. She and those old women friends of hers from church could never seem to mind their own business. It might have been even worse for me because I had everything that they wanted, but could not get.

You have always been a kind, reliable husband, while their husbands drank all their money at the shebeens. And then too, I was young and beautiful, and men were attracted to me, Phil. Something they lost when they married, but I never did. Anyway, I was explaining about that miserable day. You have no idea how terrible that day was for me – how was I to know the following days would be worse?

On that day, I made sure that when you returned, the house was spick and span – you know I am not much of a cleaner, but it was the nervous energy that got me doing all that! I was wearing that dress that got you to talk to me the very first time we met. I made your favourite meal of rice, chicken and salads with pumpkin on the side, even though it was not a Sunday. I hoped that this would help you to forgive me, maybe even forget a little and just remember the good old days when it was just you and me, but no. It was not to be.

I looked at you closely as you walked in that night from

the shebeen where you had gone to try to drown the picture of what you had seen in our bedroom earlier that day. Dear Phil, you were never much of a drinker, and generally a few glasses can drown you, but on this day, even the alcohol failed you. I could see your messenger-boy-who-dreams-to-be-a-lawyer brain asking yourself, "What makes a woman like this experiment with adultery?"

I will tell you what made me do it. And because by the time you read this I will be dead, I feel I can give you cash talk.

My husband. You are an intelligent man, even now, taking night school so that you can be a lawyer, learning what you can from your *baas* lawyer. You do not frequent Sophiatown's shebeens every day like the likes of that Can Themba, the journalist, or even Terry. You would bring your full salary home every month-end, and we would sit down and budget together to save for our future and the children we hoped to have. You would discuss with me deep stuff about the unfortunate role of the black man in today's apartheid South Africa (half the stuff I honestly did not understand). You would insist that we take our washing to the dry-cleaners because you did not want my soft hands to be destroyed by cheap soaps. You even made it a point to bring me breakfast in bed every morning before you went to work. So what made a woman like me toy with adultery? From the looks of things, you seemed like the perfect man. In fact, many women would argue that you were.

To start with, you were the only man I had ever been with.

When we married, you well know I was a virgin. Unfortunately Phil, I spent my days at home alone most of the time while you were at work, and when you sit in the house with very little to do, you start wondering what else may be out there. You wonder whether there are more sexual positions than the missionary position your husband always insists on. You wonder why many women spend ages at the communal tap talking about sex and how men are rocking their world when you have never felt anything like that. You wonder too whether all there is to conversation is stuff about the Mandelas and Sobukwes, meetings and marches on whether the authorities will care for our Sophiatown opinion when we say "we won't go", whether there is more to life than the politics of "us" and "them".

So one day you pass by Thirty-nine Steps shebeen to get a Coke in the morning, and you just feel a weird attraction to this man sitting there drinking half a jack. You smile at him, and with guts you never knew you had, you invite him to finish his drink at your place. One thing leads to another and soon, apart from making dinner for you in the evening, Phil, he is the one thing that I look forward to every morning when I wake up. (And between the two of you, I was waking up late in the mornings, worn out.)

Maybe a woman is not supposed to love only one man, but needs two to get all the qualities she needs in her perfect man. Because I loved you. I still do, even as I pen these dying words. But in some odd way, I loved and still love Terry, too.

Right from the get-go, I noticed that you and Terry were different, Phil. He is tall and fit in spite of the copious amounts of alcohol he consumes, while you are short and thin. He is dark, where you are fair, so fair some people even mistake you for a Coloured. You are serious and ambitious, Terry is funny and just happy to have a job and enough money to pay off his debts at Thirty-nine Steps. You tell me that when you look at me, I remind you of what the Greek goddess of wisdom Athena must have looked like. Terry tells me that I look better than Dolly Rathebe in those pin-ups in *Drum*. (I am sure Athena must have been something, but the only Greek woman I know is that fat woman whose husband runs the butchery, and *eish*, Phil, sometimes a woman just wants to be Dolly!) You are complicated, you speak these deep English words, but you probably could not survive Sophiatown on your own after ten. I have never heard Terry say any deep stuff, yet I know he is streetwise. You get stressed if I do not pay the rent the day you give me the money for it. Terry probably smooth-talks his way out of paying rent every other month after he has drunk it all away if his wife does not come to pick up his pay-cheque on payday. I felt secure with both of you in different ways. With you, I knew we would have a wonderful life together in old age, and with Terry, I knew when walking beside him, I was safe. Terry was always the present, Phil. The here and now. I never once considered running away with him. You, on the other hand, were my future.

Yes, Terry is a drunk. Yes, he probably is a bad husband and as a teacher, a miserable role model for the children of Sophiatown, but Phil sweetie, Terry was EXCITING.

I never had to think deeply about what I wanted to say before I opened my mouth when I was with him. With you, I am always trying to prove that yes, I read the paper. Yes, I learned a new English word today. Yes, I listened to the news on the radio. No, I am different from all these women of Sophiatown who never have both beauty and brains. Sometimes it gets tiring.

But you caught me. And it was torture. I could not believe that you would make me set a place at the table for The Suit, as a way of punishing me and ensuring that Terry could not come to retrieve his suit. It was hard at first. But soon I got used to it, particularly when you allowed me to join the social club at the church. For the first time, I had other young housewives for friends. I could share secrets and giggle with them. Some of them told me the type of bedroom stories that made me wistful for Terry. Although we continued with the routine of feeding The Suit – and one Sunday you even made me take a walk with it – I was seriously believing that you were ready to realise that I had repented, and that you would soon forgive me.

Imagine my shock then, when in spite of the extra money you gave me to entertain my friends today, you still insisted I take The Suit out, put it at the table, and feed it, like I have to do when we are just the two of us. With all those people looking at me, as if they all knew my embarrassing secret. Sure, you did not try to tell the truth when I lied about our little game by way of explaining what I was doing dishing for a suit, but still...

You humiliated me, Philemon. Yes, I admit. You got your revenge.

I cannot live with the shame. Soon the whole of Sophiatown will know about the woman who fed The Suit (Terry's wife among them). I have nothing more to live for. You have successfully killed my spirit, so what then is the body? Your joke went too far – are you still laughing?

Oh, by the way, another reason I am killing myself: I have been waiting and praying and worrying, but I cannot fool myself any longer. I am two months late.

I am pregnant, Phil. And I am not sure whether it's yours or Terry's. So I leave you both.

I wish you luck with your next wife.

Your Tilly

The Lost Suit

◆

THE DOOR CREAKED OPEN.

Doris was only two steps inside the house when she took off her stilettos. There was a thud as she threw them onto the cement floor.

"These shoes are killing me!" she grumbled. I knew better than to remind my wife about the importance of fitting shoes before buying them. It still beats me why she continued wearing the shoes when they bit her feet so much. Doris was Miss "Know-It-All" when it came to clothing items, yet she always bought wrong sizes.

Our iron bed rattled as I turned to look at my beautiful wife. She was a towering figure in our household. I had married wisely. I am a vertically challenged man with a broad frame. I made a conscious decision not to subject my offspring to eternal ridicule because of their lack of height. I had married a woman who compensated for my height deficiency. Doris had a slim body and long legs like a secretary-bird. Her plaited hair formed uneven heaps beneath her brown beret. She looked tired on this day. Her almond-shaped eyes told a story of an unpleasant day at the office – white bosses again!

"*Tjo*, these buses can be a nuisance sometimes," she said as she put her plastic bag and clipboard on the table. I concluded that bosses and buses must be related. As a clerk at the municipality offices, my wife was always having a run-in either with the frustrated clients or the white bosses who took their frustrations out on the black junior staff.

"Did they break down again?" I asked.

"I think so. Ours was more than an hour late," she said, taking one look at me and shaking her head resignedly. "I don't know how you even begin to eat in this pigsty," she mumbled, taking the broom and folding the sleeves of her blouse. It was only at that moment that I realised the floor was littered with cigarette stubs and burned matchsticks. Part of the ash had fallen into a dirty cereal bowl on the floor. "I don't know why you prefer using the floor as an ashtray," she said. At that point, I realised that anything I said would be a declaration of war. I just kept quiet and continued reading the newspaper.

"You'd better find yourself a real job," she said, starting with her uptight nonsense again. Clearly she was in the mood for a fight. I did not understand why she insisted on changing the man that I was – the man she had fallen in love with. She added in a more conversational tone, "My parents want to visit next month and you can't be lying on this bed all day when they are here."

Now I understood why she had to bring up the topic again. We discussed the issue of my profession almost every day. You never win with Doris, but I had to defend myself. "But, baby, I earn enough money for us to live on. I can even pay for your *lobola* if your parents want me to. Why all the fuss about *real* jobs now?" The only thing that made our marriage invalid in traditional terms was the fact that I had not yet paid Doris's *lobola*. Not that it was my fault anyway.

"Stompie, how many times do I have to tell you that my parents won't accept stolen money for *lobola*? If you had told me the truth from the beginning, I wouldn't be making all this *fuss* now," she said in a more condescending tone.

"But I told you the truth from day one," I stated in my defence.

"You lied to me, Stompie," she said in an amplified voice. "You told me that you were a professional, and you worked in a steel factory,"

"C'mon Doris, that's not what I said."

"What did you say?" she asked, crossing her arms on her chest while staring at me.

"I said 'I'm a steal professional, specialising in factory material.'" I said this because the clothing factories in Joburg were my main source of income. The clothes that Doris wore were from the same scheme. I did not become the best dresser in Sophiatown out of nowhere. I had a designer suit for each day of the week. I sold most of the suits to the gangs of Sophiatown, especially the group that fancied themselves as the Americans. I had never run out of cash until recently, when my connection at the factory was busted. I had to lie low for a short while.

"Why didn't you just say you were a thief?" she said that dreaded word – thief. It sounded so improper. Vulgar.

"I wouldn't think of myself as *that*," I could not even bring myself to saying the word. "I would rather refer to someone of my vocation as a re-distributor. "I don't take from black people. I only reclaim our stolen wealth from the whites who…" She interjected while I was still explaining the nature of my job.

"C'mon, Stompie, don't give me that sob story about white people who stole from your forefathers. Theft is theft, and you can't justify it." My wife never had a good grasp of the word "debate". Neither could she understand that theft is not theft when you are stealing back what has been stolen from you. She would just unleash an avalanche of accusations without listening to my point of view. I would not even try to raise my voice above hers. Instead, I chose to keep quiet and continue reading my newspaper.

"By the way, were you not supposed to attend the

meeting this evening?" she asked in a more cordial manner. It was clear that we were now past the stage of fighting about nothing. We had to discuss constructive things as husband and wife.

"What time is it?" I asked, looking at the Zobo watch sitting on a small table next to my bed. "It's a quarter past seven and the meeting was supposed to start at six."

"*Ag*, Doris, I forgot, you know," I said, trying to dismiss the idea of going to the community meeting. I was not one for "talk-talk" in any case. The learned types like the teachers, politicians and scribes from *Drum Magazine* were surely going to be there precisely to boast about their mastery of the "queen's language".

"But you can still go. You know what they say about African time," she said, trying to encourage me to attend the meeting. "You might find out that the meeting is getting started only now."

"C'mon, it's not that important. Terence is probably there anyway. I'll get the report from him," I said dismissively.

"Don't tell me about that drunk of a man. He probably forgot just like you."

"But I don't think it's really necessary to attend these meetings. Would they really demolish Sophiatown?"

"Hey, look," she said, flipping through the pages on the clipboard. She held one to my face. "This is the memo that we received today. Plans are going ahead. In about two months, this won't be our home."

"Damn! This thing is serious."

"You better get going, then."

"But why hold such an important meeting in a shebeen anyway?" I said putting on my brown pants.

"Because it can't be held anywhere else. The community hall would be an invitation for a raid by the Special Branch."

"These bloody cops!" I mumbled between breaths as I took my jacket, which was draped on the chair next to my bed. "They should mind their own business."

A cold drizzle pinched my fingers as I opened the door. I had been indoors for the entire afternoon and had not noticed the change in weather. I put on my Stetson hat, which matched my brown suit from the fashion house of Chester Barrie. Doris surveyed me up and down and shook her head.

"Why are you dressed up?" Doris knew that I had an unparalleled flair for pin-up girls. She always exercised extra caution when I went to public places alone.

"Doris, I'm going to a meeting. Do you expect me to go out in rags?"

"Just don't get drunk and pick up some pin-up girls there. Okay?"

"Stop being jealous, Doris," I said coquettishly.

"You fancy yourself far too much. Me, I'm not the jealous type!" I closed the door behind me and confronted the cold breeze.

The meeting was held at Thirty-nine Steps, a popular shebeen just a whistle away from my house in Good Street. As I walked up the stairs, there were people walking out of the shebeen in small groups of three or four. It was against the law for our kind to be found in groups of more than five. The cops, riding the *kwela-kwela* and armed with batons, torches and handcuffs, were always lurking in the dark ready to pounce. Our added nemesis was now the bulldozers lining up for the demolition of our haven – Sophiatown.

I was walking up the stairs when I heard familiar laughter inside the shebeen. It was unmistakably Terence, my brother – Thirty-nine Steps was his favourite waterhole. He had a particularly raucous laugh that had irritated the hell out of me when we were young. A little bit of brandy always brought that peculiar laughter back. Clearly, the meeting was over, but there was always a good reason to stay at Thirty-nine Steps!

My brother was in the company of friends in one corner. He sat on a sofa, a woman on his lap, holding a glass of whisky in his left hand and caressing the thigh of the woman with the right. I noticed that he hung out with his learned friends – the teachers and scribes who drank like whales. Those *okes* were known to have made drinking whisky something sacrosanct. Their resentment of people who drank "affordable" liquor was insurmountable. They referred to beer as piss that you could not even gulp down when the cops suddenly pounced.

I sheepishly made my way towards the bar, where Fatty was serving customers. Fatty, the well-endowed shebeen queen, was a no-nonsense kind of woman. All men of thirst knew better than to chisel Fatty. If you dared rub her the wrong way, you would end up with your face grotesquely distorted so that even your own mother would not recognise you. By the time she was done with you, you would be a changed man – face-lifted with extended lips, broken teeth, bleeding nose and blue eyes.

"Sis' Fatty, you know I was coming here for the meeting." I had to soften her before coming out with it.

"And you missed it. That's so irresponsible of you. I hope that yours will be the first house to be brought to the ground."

"You know, Sis' Fatty, my wife got back quite late from work because of these unreliable buses." I had to make reference to my trustworthy wife.

"Oh, that's right. I heard that the buses were running late this afternoon."

"But now that I'm here, I can't leave without wetting

my throat."

"Wetting your throat? You still owe me from last Friday, remember?"

"C'mon, Sis' Fatty, I just need two beers. I'll see you on Friday."

"Stompie, I'm getting tired of this nonsense of yours. Don't tell me that your ship hasn't sailed in on Friday, right?" She wagged a finger in my face while the other hand rested on her enormous waist.

"I promise, Sis' Fatty. I swear my eldest sister. Cut off this finger if I don't see you on Friday," I said, lifting my index finger.

"If I listened to that every time you wanted a beer, you wouldn't be having any fingers now," she said, pushing two beers towards me.

"Sis' Fatty, you are the greatest!" She flashed a lopsided grin. I knew she took the remark as a compliment that had nothing to do with her huge girth.

Beads of cold dripped down the beer bottles. I grabbed my two companions and took a cursory look around the house. I went to the furthest corner where there was an empty table. I filled the glass with half beer and half foam. Doing things in haste has its disadvantages. I had to wait for the foam to disappear before I could drink my beer peacefully. I slugged the first glass in two gulps and poured another.

After taking a sip from the second glass, the music got louder. The popular sounds of "Hamba Nontsokolo" by Dorothy Masuka were blaring from the gramophone. Suddenly the dance floor was filled with men and women wiggling, wriggling and tapping to the song. Everything was done rhythmically.

One of the fringe benefits of not having ostrich legs is that you are fast on your feet. Both men and women knew that you needed a partner to occupy the stage. I took to the periphery of the dance floor, hoping that my moves would be noticed.

Just like in the unimaginative Cinderella stories, a beauty came out of nowhere and danced with me. She wore a white blouse with black dots, a long blue skirt and white shoes. She had long plaited hair, yellow skin and sparkling black eyes. Her teardrop earrings glittered under the lights. She had high cheekbones, small pink lips and a pointed chin.

She held her skirt on the sides, kicking this way and that. I curled my arm under hers and we moved towards centre stage. I went down on my knees and started patting her ankles, gradually working my way up her legs, around her hips – I stayed a little longer around the hips. All of Thirty-nine Steps went berserk. There was ululating, whistling and screaming as she moved away and blew me a kiss. We rejoined and I repeated the motions, with the rest of the revellers now watching. I gradually moved up, touching her until we were almost level. We would have been level except that I was not exactly the same height as her. Some perverts call a match between a vertically challenged man and a long-boned woman "if" – each letter representing the man and the woman respectively.

It was now her turn. By the time she got to my waist, my crotch had swollen to irrepressible proportions. We danced like we had been practising together – the bulge in my pants not withstanding. Before the end of the song she blew another kiss in my direction, and I took that as an invitation that we would meet later.

After gulping down the remainder of my beer, my eyes circulated in all corners of Thirty-nine Steps in search of my beautiful dance partner. She was nowhere to be found. With newly acquired bravado, I moved to the table where my brother and his friends were busy discussing the passive resistance movement. I was not interested in intellectual or political debates. I just wanted to be in a strategic position to scout for the beauty – my beautiful dance partner had suddenly vanished.

The brandy on the table was still on the shoulders, but my brother saw it was necessary to get another one in my honour. Terence called on Fatty: "I need some hooch for my brother here!" he said with a glimmer of liquor-induced generosity. "This man dances like nobody's business," he added boisterously.

"I've never seen that child before. Who is she?"

"You know me, man," I said, taking off my hat and putting it on the table in front of me. "I get such nice childs all the time, I didn't even ask her name."

"From now on, she's the dancing queen and you are the king, my brother."

"Try vanishing queen, maybe. I haven't seen her since we left the dance floor."

At that moment Fatty brought a half-jack, and I wasted no time slugging it. More alcohol flowed until the lights, the tables, the bottles and the glasses started dancing synchronically in front of me.

Beer in hand, I staggered towards the door. It was not time to go yet. Who can be bothered to go back to a nagging woman when free alcohol is flowing from all directions? I just needed to take a leak. I balanced on the rails as I went down the thirty-nine steps. Down on the street, I emptied my bladder against the nearest tree. It was a long beer-filled piss. I zipped my pants and as I turned, *voila*! There was the dancing queen, standing under the street lamp, shivering with cold. I had no option but to change my mind about going back to Thirty-nine Steps. Nothing can be better than landing a hot child after slugging a cold beer on a rainy day.

"Hey, beautiful, are you going already?" I asked, bearing in mind that there had been no time for formal introductions earlier.

"I was supposed to have gone a while back, but the man who was supposed to pick me up is not here yet," she responded, in a somewhat shaky voice.

"This is callous disregard of your beauty and dignity as a woman. It's a travesty of human justice. Such a creature does not deserve to be called a man!" It was the hooch speaking.

"That's true," she concurred even though she probably didn't understand half of what I had just said. The important thing was that in front of her was a man who seemed to care about her.

"Is he supposed to be your boyfriend?"

"Well, from this moment on he's my ex-boyfriend."

"That serves him right. How far is your place from here?"

"Victoria Road, just around the corner. I'm just scared to walk alone."

"It is a sin before the eyes of the Creator to allow a beautiful girl like you to walk alone at night. Stompie cannot allow that!" I said, thumping my chest.

"Are you sure about this?" she asked in a melodious voice.

"My darling, I'm deliriously in love with you. I'd do anything to make you happy." I took off my jacket and covered her head and shoulders with it. I tried to take calculated steps to minimise my staggers.

"Thanks, Stompie, you are so kind. I live by myself and it gets very lonely sometimes." I wrapped my arm around her waist. She wrapped hers around mine.

"You'll be living alone no more," I assured her. No

beautiful woman can claim loneliness in the presence of Stompie.

"But how come I've never seen you at Thirty-nine Steps before?"

"I don't get out of my place too often. Only on special days," she said.

"And what's the occasion today?"

"It's my birthday," she said, with a glimmer of excitement.

"It's your birthday today? Stompie will make this a special one for you."

There was a momentary pause. The next time she spoke, it was on a different matter. "I thought your dance was impressive for a man of your height," she said, releasing a slight giggle. I took that as a compliment. I knew my prowess on the dance floor would do wonders.

"My lack of height is compensated for in more ways than one, believe me," I said, assuring her of the vastness of my talents.

"But I'm sure there are things you can't reach because of your height," she said, a mischievous smile playing at the corners of her mouth.

"There's nothing I can't do," I said, moving closer to her face. "I can even reach your lips," I said in a half-whisper and planted a kiss on her soft lips. She welcomed it by slightly parting them. It was a breathtaking tongue-locking kiss. My hands fumbled on her curved backside before she pushed me away. "Not here," she said and looked away timidly.

"By the way, my name is Candy." I was a bit embarrassed that I had forgotten to ask her name. Anyway, I had my priorities straight. I had to score that night, and I was about to score really big.

"Candy? What a beautiful name. No wonder your lips

are so sweet and tender."

"So it's my lips that you wanted to taste?" She had a devilish smile on her face.

"I really liked your dance moves, especially when you wiggled your hips."

"I like your suit. I'd love to see it hung at my place," she said, thus giving me a passport to her bedroom.

"I like your style, Candy." The brandy had circulated past all the filters in my body. My head was spinning. My eyes saw things in double. My legs were rubbery and I walked like a newly born calf. I leaned heavily on her, trying to balance. I just wanted to hang on until we got to her place.

When I came to, darkness had enveloped my surroundings. A frog croaked not too far from my ear. Dogs barked in the distance. There was the distinctive sound of an owl hooting nearby. I shuddered. I was lying face-down with my naked buttocks facing heavenwards. Goosebumps covered my skin. My ears, fingers and feet were frozen. My entire back was covered with dew. My nose was clogged. The owl hooted again. I got up, both hands covering my crotch, and headed in the direction of the dogs. I tripped over a heap of soil and landed on my chest. The grass was wet. I got up and jumped over more heaps.

I had to get to the nearest house before the early-morning workers started making their way to the bus station. I raised clouds of dust behind me as I sprinted across the streets of Sophiatown. Although my legs were wobbly, they managed to take me to my brother's place in Edith Street. I knew he would be fast asleep after the previous night's drinking. I went around the house to the side of his bedroom. Panting and hissing with exhaustion, I knocked on his window. "Terence, Terence! It's me, open up," I shouted desperately. But there was no answer. "Terence, please open up. It's me – Stompie. Please open up."

Someone peeped through a slit in the curtains. The curtain was then drawn to the side, and Grace, my brother's wife, appeared in the window, looking like she had seen a ghost. "Please open!" I pleaded with her.

"What happened?" she shouted back, pointing to my lower limbs. I was then reminded of my nakedness. I put both my hands in front in an attempt to cover what she had already seen. She beckoned me to go to the door.

"Where have you been? Doris was looking for you the whole night," she shouted at me after opening the door. She was already in her white nurse's uniform. "Don't tell me you left your clothes at some naughty boy's home, because that won't hold," she said, shouting at me like I was a small boy. "Terence, here's your good-for-nothing brother!" She called to her husband, who was in the other room. I knew Terence would be more sympathetic because he had been through a similar experience before and I had come to his rescue, in a way. "I'll explain what happened," I said between coughs.

Terence emerged from the bedroom. He had a bare chest and his pants were folded up to his knees. His upper body was spotted with white soap bubbles, and he had a washing rag in his hand. "Grace, can't you see that he's cold?" He reminded his wife that he was the one who wore the pants in the household.

"Here," Grace handed me a blanket, "cover yourself with this." The nurse in her still cared after all.

It was only at that moment that I realised my teeth were chattering, and my whole body was shivering with cold.

"Please prepare something hot for him," my brother said.

"He'll have to explain what happened. I'm not gonna lie to Doris. She's been worried sick about him." She talked as if I was not there or I was totally deaf.

"Grace, my brother is dying and all you have to talk about is his wife!" My brother seemed to be reading my mind. I kept wiping my running nose with the back of my hand. I desperately needed something to warm me up.

Grace lit the coal stove and made me sit in front of it. She gave me vegetable soup after heating it on the stove. I felt a bit of relief, but I didn't want Grace to notice this.

"I was robbed," I tried to explain to Grace.

"C'mon, no one would even dream of robbing a *tsotsi* like you. Tell me what happened, or else I'll find out for myself at Thirty-nine Steps," said Grace, who was probably the great grand-daughter of Thomas from the biblical narratives.

"Grace, what have you become now – some Sophiatown private investigator?" Terence intervened in my defence.

"I'm no private investigator. All I want is the truth." It was getting warm and my body was welcoming the heat. I pretended to fall asleep in front of the coal stove.

"I can see he's falling asleep now. I want all the information when I come back from work this afternoon," said Grace.

My reprieve came when she finally left. "Come sleep over here," my brother said, calling me to his bedroom. "Put on these clothes when you get up." He showed me an old shirt and a pair of jeans. "All right, the woman is gone now. Tell me, my brother, what happened exactly?"

I had to tell him the truth because he was the only person who was sure to be on my side. He had that obligation, that's what brothers do.

"Man, I really don't know what happened."

"What do you mean, you don't know?"

"I met this child at Thirty-nine Steps last night and she took me to her place."

"Where's the place?"

"She said Victoria Street. I must have sunk into a blackout because I don't know how I got there, but what I know is that when I woke up I was in an open field, naked!"

"You mean you slept stark naked outside?"

"That's all I can remember. And I can't go home without the lost suit. You know what Doris is like." My wife always scrutinised my clothing, especially after I had paid a visit to a shebeen. I had to explain each and every stain, especially those that looked like lipstick. She could smell women's perfume on my clothes miles away.

"Okay, listen, I've got to go to work right now," he said, glancing at his wristwatch. "Try to get some sleep and we'll look for your suit when I get back."

"All right. I'm really tired right now." The truth of the matter is that I didn't know whether Candy had taken the suit, or if she herself was a victim. Something worse could have happened to her.

I was dazed when I woke up from my slumber. My face felt numb and swollen. I took a hand-mirror from the small table next to my brother's bed: my eyes were red and my uncombed hair pointed to the ceiling. I lit the coal stove and filled the kettle with water. When the water boiled, I bathed, using my brother's towels. I looked at the threadbare jeans that he left for me, and thought he must be crazy. How could the best dresser of Sophiatown wear such rags? I went to his wardrobe to see if he had a brown suit that resembled my lost one. I couldn't find any. I took his blue suit instead and put it on. The pants were loose-fitting and I had to fasten the belt above the bellybutton.

In the top left pocket of the jacket I found a monthly bus ticket and a ten-shilling note. I was hit by a sudden brainwave and the compass in my head pointed to town. I had to find a similar-looking suit before Doris came back from work. It was Thursday, Sheila's Day, and I knew the maids would be streaming into the city centre. Thursdays were the only day of the week when maids (mostly called Sheila by their bosses) would be found roaming the streets buying groceries and running errands for their white bosses.

I went to the bus terminus in Victoria Street and hopped on a bus to town. The bus was empty. The majority of our people had no reason to go to town at midday on a Thursday. Those few who did visited the Native Affairs Department to apply for passes and work permits. The bus rocked its way along the Mayfair circle, roared up Hurst hill and glided into town. As we drove along Market Street, I spotted a number of Sheilas, still in their kitchen uniforms, heading towards the bus station.

I spotted a sign that read "Henry's Dry-Cleaners". With launderers around, there was the exciting prospect of hooking up with one of the washerwomen. "Hold it there, driver!" I shouted. The driver hit the brake pedal furiously, and the bus came to a screeching halt. He looked at me in disgust, his nostrils flaring, but he opted not to utter a word. No one messes with Stompie, the gangster of Sophiatown. I got off, leaving a not-so-pleased bus driver behind.

I wandered along Market Street just to make sure that there was no *mkatakata*. There was a single cop patrolling the area. I averted my eyes as he looked my direction. I went into Henry's Dry-Cleaners and started frantically searching all pockets of my brother's jacket. "Damn! I left the dry-clean slip," I mumbled to myself before leaving the premises. In front of me was a white man with a brown suit tucked under his arm. A closer look told me that it was the same label as mine, a Chester Barrie!

I tailed the white man, hoping that he would make the mistake of walking in the smaller streets. I would sweep him with two feet and send him flying. I maintained a reasonable distance so I would not lose track of him, and also not to cause alarm. He went towards a green Buick parked on the side of the road. He opened it and put the suit in the back seat before leaving in haste. I noticed that he did not lock the car. But the trouble was the patrolling cop.

I had to act swiftly. I took a quick look at the white man and saw him heading towards the bank. I lit a cigarette and started puffing with ease, as I walked towards the cop with a swagger often displayed by rich guys. "Hey brother," I called in a fake American accent. The white cop lifted his head to look at me with undisguised contempt. He had a bushy moustache, grey eyes and a double chin.

"Do you mind looking after my suit on the back seat there? I'm just going back to the bank to find my keys."

That sent the white cop into a frenzy: "*Wat*?" he blurted out. "Who do you think you are? *Ek is die baas hiersô. Ek is nie jou vriend nie!*" He was quick to state categorically that he was the boss, and not a friend of mine.

I pressed a little further. "I'll be back in a jiffy, Officer. I left my keys at the bank when I went to exchange foreign currency," I said, blowing rings of smoke in his direction.

"*Luister hiersô, jong!*" he said, wagging a finger in my face. "I don't care if you come from the United bloody States of America. You are still a *kaffir*!"

"Officer, you don't have to insult me. I'm asking you to look after my suit, that's all," I explained calmly. His face turned red.

"Why don't you take your bloody suit and go?" he barked.

"Never mind, brother. I ain't got no problem taking my suit," I said, taking it from the back seat. I closed the door behind me and walked briskly towards the bank. I glanced behind me and saw the unsuspecting cop still patrolling the area. I went past the bank and opened my parcel as soon as I turned the corner. It was just the jacket without any trousers!

I went back to the dry-cleaners and shouted at them. "The *baas* is furious that you guys only gave him the jacket. He sent me to get the pants," I said, producing the jacket covered in a transparent plastic cover. The old Jewish woman behind the counter had a pair of glasses resting on the bridge of her nose. She looked at me over her glasses as if I was mad. "Who?" she asked, looking at me quizzically.

"My master, he says you didn't give him the pants," I protested.

"Which master, you mean Mr Williams from 49 Princess Street?" she asked, squinting as she read the small piece of paper. It had to be him.

"Can I have a look?" I extended my hand across the counter. She handed the piece of paper to me. I read the details and nodded in agreement. "Yes, that's him. You only gave him the jacket," I launched another missile, trying to steal her attention away from the piece of paper.

"Sir, we told your master that the trousers were not ready yet. We had to stitch them up before dry-cleaning," she said matter-of-factly.

"Oh, is that so," I said, trying to think of a recourse. "But can you give me the pants? Because he needs them urgently," I said, surreptitiously slipping the piece of paper into my pocket.

"Why didn't he say so?" she enquired irritably. "He'll have to bring the slip. No slip, no clothes. He knows that's our policy."

"All right, I'll tell him then. But he won't be too pleased with this." I left in fury and went around the block, glancing behind me repeatedly. I mused over the idea of paying a quick visit to the white man's house at Princess Street.

Across the street was a post office where I could make a phone call. I felt the piece of paper in my pocket before making a dash across the street. I took a cursory glance around before taking it out and dialling the number on it. The phone rang several times and no one picked up. Their Sheila was probably out gossiping with the other maids. I dialled again and it rang twice before someone picked up the receiver.

"Hullo!" A woman's voice greeted on the other side.

"Hullo, Ma'am, I'm Mpisto from Henry's Dry-Cleaners. Is Mr Williams in?" I had to use a name that was easy to remember.

"No, Sir. The *baas* is not home." I gathered that she was a domestic worker, the Sheila of the white bosses, and my key to the house.

"What a pity. We wanted to apologise for the delay in fixing the trousers."

"He only arrives at about seven in the evening,"

"The trousers are ready now. We'll ask one of our employees to collect the slip."

"He'll have to come when the *baas* is home." Her stubbornness was putting a spanner in the wheels. This warranted a change in tactics.

"I see. What's your name?" I had to think fast.

"Lenah, the domestic worker."

"Lenah, what a lovely name." I spoke in a low voice.

"Thank you," she said, with a slight giggle.

"How come you are at work on a Thursday? Your husband must be lonely."

"I am not married," she said.

"You are not married?" I exclaimed. "I must see you today. I'll marry you if you are as beautiful as your voice," I said in a seductive voice.

"I don't know about that," she was giggling uncontrollably now.

"Maybe I should come over there personally so we can talk about this."

"Heh, I don't know," she said with a bit of coyness, "Maybe."

"I'll be there before six."

"If you come before six, I'll still be alone."

It took me another hour or so to reach 49 Princess Street. The house was humungous. This Mr Williams must be something big, I said to myself. There could definitely be benefits to a relationship with Lenah. I pressed the bell, and Lenah responded.

"Hi, Lenah, it's me, Mpisto."

"Hi, Mpisto," she said excitedly. "I'll be there now." Within no time Lenah appeared. She was a large woman, probably in her thirties. She wore a pink overall and matching headscarf. Skin-lightening creams had left her with huge dark patches on her cheeks. She smiled as soon as she saw me, exposing the so-called passion gap in her front teeth. She unlocked the padlock and let me in. "Come this side," she said, leading me to a narrow passage that took us to the maid's quarters behind the main house. As I walked behind her, I watched her bums moving up and down in a jigsaw-like motion. Somehow her ample behind made her quite desirable.

The stench of rotten food assailed me as she opened the door. The room was dark, save for the small flicker of light that came through the pigeonhole of a window. She switched the light on and there was a stampede of cockroaches as they ran for cover.

"Welcome to my palace," Lenah said with a wide grin across her plump face.

"Thank you," I said because it was a polite thing to say. Clearly, Lenah and I had different notions of a palace. She did everything in this "palace". In one corner there was a primus stove, on which sat a small shiny pot. Next to it was a bucket filled with water and a small plastic washing basin. On the foot of her bed was a bar of cracked green soap. On the table sat an enamel plate with a mountain of food. Her wet bloomers and washing rag were on a washing-line that ran across the room.

The sight of her undergarments made me realise the depth of my mistake. I could fit both my legs into one leg of her bloomers. I swear, if elephants wore undergarments, they would wear the same size as Lenah.

"Sit here," she said, ushering me to the bed as if there was another place to sit. I sat down and my eyes darted from one corner to another. The room had no ceiling. The corrugated sheets of the bare roof were dripping with dark liquid. We sat quietly next to each other. She kept taking cautious glances at me. I had to show some affection.

"You are more beautiful than I had imagined," I said, charming my way into her heart. She smiled from ear to ear, pleased with what she was hearing.

"I'm glad you think so," she said as she played with her fingers. A momentary silence followed.

"I think you are handsome too," she said, as if she felt under obligation to return the compliment. She tilted her head towards me and rested her hand on my thigh. I closed my eyes and kissed her. The brazen business of getting intimate with a woman that I did not have feelings for was something that I just had to learn. These are the sacrifices that we menfolk have to make sometimes. You just close your eyes and imagine you are with a woman that you desire. I did not have the slightest feeling for Lenah, but I had to play along, if only to save my marriage. I had to find those trousers, whatever it cost.

"Let me take off my uniform," she said, and got up. She removed her headscarf, revealing her uncombed hair. Underneath the pink overall she had on a floral blouse and a long, brown skirt. She took off her blouse, exposing folds of flesh that dangled before my eyes. She had a cream petticoat on underneath her skirt. Seeing Lenah half-naked was a ghastly sight. I had to take control of the situation, or she would start asking things that she had no business asking. "So, Mr Williams arrives after seven?" I decided to casually raise the question of the *baas* as she was busy taking off her kitchen uniform.

"If at all," she responded without even looking at me. "Sometimes there are emergencies and he is forced to travel." That did not sound good. I was just hoping that today was not one of those days he had to travel.

"Emergencies. That sounds serious. What kind of work does he do?"

"He's a police superintendent," she said, clearly not understanding the panic that she instilled in me with this bit of information. If she was looking at me, she might have noticed that I was visibly startled.

"I see," I said meekly. I made a mental note that this was not the place to ever spend a night. At that moment, a car hooted outside. Lenah jumped up and grabbed her overall and headscarf. "That must be the *baas*!" she blurted out.

"Just check if he's got the dry-clean slip." I didn't know whether she had heard me, because by the time I finished the sentence she was outside already. I heard the gate screech and the sound of the car driving in. Moments later, the vehicle drove off again and Lenah closed the gate.

"The coast is clear," she announced calmly. She held a

parcel wrapped in a plastic bag.

"What do you mean?" I wondered.

"The *baas* is gone. The house will be ours for the rest of the weekend." I imagined spending the entire weekend trapped between Lenah's enormous thighs. She would drain all my energy, and I might still have to go home without the suit in the end.

"He didn't even get out of the car," she said, and handed me a spoon. She dipped into the *pap* that swam in a greasy stew, which probably contained limbs of cockroaches. Like a dog feeding on human excrement, I had to look ahead and eat what was in front of me without registering it in my mind. I took one bite, and all the food I had eaten earlier wanted to vacate my stomach immediately. Eating that food was more unpalatable than drinking dirty water after washing the dishes.

"But he brought this," she said, showing me the plastic bag. I opened it, and to my pleasant surprise, he had collected the trousers.

"Oh Lenah, this is great!" I grabbed and kissed her. My tongue slipped through the gap in her front teeth. It was only then that I understood why it was called the passion gap. Her hand started fumbling around my belt and I pulled back instantly. "Eh, is there somewhere where I can get a cigarette?"

"A cigarette at this time?" She looked at me as if I had taken leave of my senses.

"I'm craving one. I just cannot fall asleep without a puff."

"It's too late now. There are no corner shops here."

"C'mon, Lenah, I just can't sleep without having a smoke," I said, shivering like a junkie. She threw up her hands, hissing in exasperation. "Okay, I'll check in the *baas*'s drawer." As soon as she left, I grabbed the jacket and the pants and swiftly made my way to the back of the property. I climbed over the fence and landed with a thud on the other side. I made a dash for the street under the cover of darkness, leaving white people's dogs barking behind long fences. There was a flicker of headlights and I took a dive to the ground until it went past. It was a big green *kwela-kwela*, with police officers looking through the mesh windows in quest of a stray black man. A black man fleeing with a parcel tucked under his arm in the middle of town at night could make a perfect shooting target!

The van drove past and once it was safely out of sight, I got up and continued running. When I got to Park Station, I collapsed on a bench in utter exhaustion. I was heaving, trying to gasp every bit of air. The commuters surrounded me, wondering what had happened to the "servant of the lord". Drenched in sweat, I explained that I was being chased by some *tsotsis* who were after my suit. My fellow travellers celebrated my survival, because those merciless *tsotsis* might have killed me for my expensive suit. I explained that I had to change into the new suit so that the *tsotsis* would not be able to identify me, lest they were still following.

I got off at the bus station in Sophiatown dressed in my brown suit and carrying my brother's blue suit in a plastic bag. I was content with the acquisition of "my lost suit", but this was not enough to assuage the agonising prospect of having to deal with a jealous wife at home. As I came closer to the house, I noticed that the lights were on, which suggested that Doris was still awake. Her jealousy would not let her go to sleep!

I knocked timidly, and without a response, the doorknob turned and my wife appeared. I always told her to ask for the person's identity, and not just to open the door at night. She always argued that she only did this to me, and that she knew my knock distinctively.

"Hey, Doris," I greeted her with a reluctant grin on my face, "I'm back." I am not sure why I had to announce my arrival, but somehow I felt the need to do so.

"Welcome back, Stompie," she said and turned away, grim-faced. Behind her I saw my nervous-looking brother seated next to his wife, who stared at me with disgust.

"Hey, guys," I greeted them casually.

"Hey, brother," my brother said. The women kept quiet. I decided to take a seat next to Terence.

"So, how did the meeting go?" For a moment I did not know what Doris was talking about. She got up and went to the bedroom.

"The meeting?" I repeated her words thoughtlessly. I was glad that she was not looking at me.

"Yes, the meeting that you were going to when we last spoke yesterday evening," she yelled from the bedroom.

"Oh, that." I had not given myself enough time to think about an explanation. "You know, Doris, there was a raid at Thirty-nine Steps last night."

"Is that so?" There was a twinge of sarcasm in her voice.

"Yes, we were picked up by a *kwela-kwela*. We spent last night and the whole afternoon today behind bars." As I spoke, Grace was staring at me with her piercing eyes.

"I'm glad your suit was not damaged in the process. What did they take you in for?" Doris's probing was becoming problematic, and I knew something was up.

"For not possessing passes," I duly explained.

"That's funny, Stompie, because your pass is here."

"It's here?" I felt cornered. "I knew I had left it somewhere in the house," I said in my defence.

"As a matter of fact, you left it in the same jacket that you were wearing yesterday." She came out of the bedroom with the suit I lost the previous night, hanging from a wire hanger.

"How, eh, where did you get that from?" To say I was perplexed would be an understatement. I was tongue-tied with shock and embarrassment.

"Is this suit yours, Stompie?" There was no evading the question. The suit was exactly the one I had worn the previous day. I nodded. "It looks like it, Doris," I found myself muttering.

"Then, how come you are wearing a different suit today?"

"Where did you lose your suit?" Grace interjected. My sister-in-law's loathing for me was no secret.

"I got this one in town." They all knew where I got my suits from. But the trouble was to explain how I lost my other suit, which they now had in their possession.

"Grace!" My brother added his voice to the fracas, "Let's leave Stompie and Doris to sort this matter out."

"We went to get your suit, Stompie," Grace said, ignoring Terence's plea.

"We found your suit hanging on the cross of a grave," Doris said, adding to the chaos.

"A grave? Whose grave?" I wondered in bewilderment.

"Candy's grave," responded Grace.

"Grace!" Terence grabbed his wife's hand, trying to persuade her to leave.

"Leave me alone!" she shouted at her husband as she shook her hand free from his grip. "This low-life brother of yours is a pathological liar!" I got up and charged towards her. "Did you just call me a low-life?"

"You thought you'd make a fool out of Doris forever? We got you this time, brother. No more pin-up girls for you."

"That's it. It's time to go now," said Terence, opening the door and pulling Grace outside.

"Doris doesn't know how to handle cheats like him. I wanted to teach him a lesson." Her voice was drowned by the darkness of the night, and I was left to deal with Doris, who was legendary for sustaining such tirades.

"Did you hear that she just called me a cheat?"

"You are a cheat, Stompie. We've just proved it."

"You've just proved it? Doris, what's going on?" I asked with devastation.

"What's going on about what?" she asked, drawing out a chair to sit. I took the chair opposite her. "Did you and Grace set me up?"

"There's no conspiracy, Stompie. I told you to stay away from pin-up girls."

"But why is she saying she wanted to teach me a lesson?" I asked.

"I don't know," she shrugged.

"Doris, all of this is getting me confused. How does my suit get associated with graves?" I pried, genuinely curious, because things were not adding up for me.

"We went to Thirty-nine Steps and were told that you were last seen dancing with an unknown girl. Terence said that you had told him that the girl was from Victoria Street. When we got there, it was just a cemetery. And we found your suit draped on the cross of Candy's grave," she explained.

"I don't understand. How do you know it was Candy's grave?" I was hearing words, speaking words, but nothing made sense.

"Look," she said, opening her handbag. She unfolded a small piece of paper. "This is the inscription on the grave." I took the piece of paper and read:

Candy Snyman
Born on 4 September 1918

Died tragically on
13 February 1948

My mouth was left agape. "So, Candy is dead?" I said, not asking anybody in particular.

"It looks like she's been dead for seven years now," Doris said, matter-of-factly. "Apparently she was killed by a guy who picked her up from Thirty-nine Steps."

I wondered how it was possible that of all the pin-up girls who filled Thirty-nine Steps, I would choose a ghost. Death has a tendency to choose the prettiest of women. That child was just too beautiful to lie in the loneliness of a grave.

"But Doris," I said, taking her hand, feeling calmer as I realised I had found another leaf to hide under. She lifted her eyes and looked at me in wonderment.

"Are you jealous of a ghost?"

PART TWO

White Encounters

White Encounters

◆

"THE DOCTOR SAYS YOU must say 'Ahhh!'" my mother interpreted for me.

"Ahhh!" I said.

"You must open your mouth wide when you say 'Ahhh!'"

"Ahhh…" I said, opening my mouth very wide. My mouth was dry.

The doctor gripped my jaw tightly. His hands were smooth and cold. He then shone something that looked like a torch into my mouth. I closed my eyes because the light was blindingly bright. There was a sour liquid in my mouth. The doctor said something in his tongue, gently tapping me on my shoulder.

"Sipho, the doctor says you must get up now," my mother said, also tapping me on my shoulder. I opened my eyes and saw the doctor holding a rotten tooth with pliers. He threw it into an enamel basin. The basin sat on a trolley draped with a green cloth. There were many tools in the basin. They all looked shiny.

Earlier that day, while sitting on the benches outside the doctor's house, a nurse had come pushing a trolley. She put on white gloves and took out a long needle from the basin. She injected many people. Some children cried, and their mothers held them tightly as the nurse injected them. There was a man with a swollen face. He could not open his mouth wide. The nurse touched his face, trying to make him open his mouth. The man groaned and kicked in the air, frightening everyone around. Other men jumped in and held him to the ground. The nurse injected him and he stopped groaning. My mother told me not to be scared because my tooth was not that bad. The nurse came to me and asked which tooth was troubling me. My mother told her, and she told me to open my mouth. She injected me with something that made my mouth numb. I pinched my cheeks several times, but I felt no pain.

"Mama, is that my tooth?" I said, pointing at the rotten tooth. My tongue was rubbery. My voice sounded strange to my own ears. There was something like cotton stashed in my mouth.

"Yes, it's your tooth, my boy. You did very well," she said, taking me by the hand and leading me outside. There were many people still sitting on the benches outside. There were adults who went there with children my age, just like my mother and I. There were also adults who went there by themselves. The adults who went there alone looked sick. Some had scarves wrapped around their faces and others had swollen faces.

"You mean he took out my tooth already?"

"Yes, you were strong, my boy. Now you are a man," she said.

"You mean the white man made me a man by taking out my tooth?"

"Yes, you are a man because you endured the pain of extracting a tooth."

"Does this mean I don't need to circumcise any more, Mama?"

"No, you are still gonna go for circumcision. Now, don't talk too much. Your gums are gonna bleed and it will be painful."

"But I don't feel any pain, Mama."

"Come spit here," she said, opening the lid of a rubbish

bin. I took the cotton wool out of my mouth. It was drenched in a mixture of blood and saliva. I threw the cotton wool into the rubbish bin. I then spat a gush of blood.

"You see, so much blood. That's why you must keep your mouth shut now." I nodded my head. I felt the pulse of my veins in the gaping hole in my mouth. We walked, my mother and I, across the town, not saying much to each other. It was hot, but we walked under the shade of trees that hugged the road. Cars whizzed past. We went past tall buildings that looked like they were going to fall on us. We saw white people's children holding bags full of books. They were wearing hats, striped school blazers and grey pants, or tunics in the case of girls. Some waved at us. We crawled up the hill. The 1820 Settlers' Monument gazed at us from the top of a hill on the opposite side of town. The structure looked like a ship that had been dropped from the sky. I was getting tired.

"Are we going home, Mama?"

"No, son, we are going to work."

"I am too tired to work."

"What I mean is that I am just going to my work place with you."

"What do you do at your work place, Mama?"

"You shall see," she said, and then added, "Come, let me carry you." She picked me up and carried me on her back. "Sit still, okay? I'm tired, don't jump on my back!"

We walked until we got to a big white house surrounded by trees. My mother put me down. She then took out a key from her handbag and unlocked the gate. We entered the house through the kitchen door. The house had glossy tiles and I could hear people in another room talking in a strange tongue. We entered a small room and my mother changed into a yellow kitchen uniform. She spread a blanket on the small sofa in the room.

"Here, try to sleep, okay?" she said, and I nodded.

When I woke up, I was alone in the room. My face felt strange and my right eye wouldn't open properly. There was pain in my mouth. My head felt heavy and inflated. The sound of heavy footsteps coming from outside the room stole my attention. The footsteps were unmistakably my mother's. A child giggled. The footsteps drew closer and went past the room. They came back and went down the corridor again. The child continued to giggle. I figured that my mother was giving the child a ride on her back, a game I liked. I got up, hoping that I would also get a ride. I stood at the door and I saw my mother in full stride running down the corridor with a white child on her back. When she got to the end of the corridor, she turned back and ran towards me. Her brow glittered with sweat. I felt embarrassed on behalf of my mother.

"Hey, Sipho, you are up?" my mother said. She was heaving with exhaustion. I did not respond. I was still shocked to see my mother carrying a white boy on her back and running as fast as she could. She sheepishly put him down.

"This is Mark," she said and turned to the white boy. She said something to him in white people's tongue. I heard her saying my name while talking to the white boy. The white boy smiled. He was the same height as me. His hair was carefully trimmed. He had grey eyes, a round face, a pointed nose and a double chin. He had a toy car in his hand.

"Do you wanna play with Mark?" my mother asked.

"Does he know how to talk?" I asked my mother.

"He speaks English. He will teach you."

"What is English?"

"It is white people's tongue."

"Why doesn't he speak our tongue?" At that point, she

turned to the white boy and spoke in the supposed white people's tongue. The boy replied, looking at me as if he was addressing me directly. He then turned and ran down the passage.

"Mark wants to be friends with you," my mother reported. "You are both six years old. He'll also be starting school soon." I wondered what kind of game I would play with a white boy whose tongue I didn't understand. Mark came back with toys in a small bag. He took out cars, guns, Superman and other toys.

"*Vrityo, vrityo, vrityo,*" or at least what I heard Mark saying sounded more or less like that. He pushed a toy car towards me. He drove another one, making the familiar sounds, "Voom-voom-voom!" That, at least, was a tongue I understood very well. Mark and I played, using physical gestures to communicate. If I did not understand something, I would look at my mother. She would then tell me what Mark was saying. Mark did the same. My mother soon had to abandon her job as the referee in my game with Mark so she could continue with her chores in the house. We played, Mark and I, while my mother was busy cleaning the house.

I could hear my mother talking to someone else. It was a woman. They spoke in the white people's tongue. Their voices drew closer. It was a white woman. She came into our room and shouted something at us. Mark shook his head and lowered his eyes. She stretched her arm to pick him up, but Mark ignored her and continued driving his car. The white woman turned to my mother. Her face contorted, and then she shouted at my mother. Then she pointed at me and Mark, still shouting. My mother repeatedly said something that sounded like, "I'm sorry, Madam." The white woman wagged her finger in my mother's face, the finger then pointed in my direction, and then at the door. She then grabbed Mark by his wrist and dashed out of the room.

My mother took off the yellow headscarf and overall. She folded them nicely and put them back where she got them when we had arrived in the morning. She kept wiping below her eyes with the back of her hand.

"Mama, are you crying?" I asked, as I noticed the tears streaming down her face.

"No, my boy. Mama is not crying," she said, speaking in a suppressed voice.

"But how come you have tears on your face?"

"I'm just sweating, my boy. It's not tears." At that moment, she burst out crying openly. I hugged her thigh, and felt tears streaming out of my eyes too. I didn't know why my mother was hurting, but I cried alongside her. She took out her handkerchief and wiped my tears.

"Let's go, my boy," she said, taking her handbag. I remembered to take my new possession with me. "No, leave that."

"But it's mine, Mama,"

"I know, just leave it."

"But Mark gave me the car. It is mine," I protested.

"Don't worry, I'll buy you another one," she said. I thought this was unreasonable. We walked out of the room and Mark was standing at the door of his room. He waved his pink fingers at me as I went out through the kitchen door with my mother. I waved back before getting out of the house.

We walked across the town. We passed many shops selling different things. We got to a place where there were many buses and many people. Some people were standing in long queues. We joined one of the queues. Women stood on the roadside selling apples, bananas, tomatoes and potatoes. A woman came with a shiny pot and opened it in front of us, shouting that they were fresh. I stretched my neck and looked in the pot and saw sheep heads. They looked like they were smiling. She pointed to another woman on the other side of the road, who was busy turning sheep heads on a fire, and said they had just been prepared there. My mother looked the other way.

We boarded the bus. Another woman waved at my mother.

"Come sit here next to me, wife of my cousin," the woman said, inviting us to share the seat with her. She was large and had taken the greater part of the seat.

"Thank you, mother of Khaya," said my mother.

"Who is this handsome man you are with today?" the woman asked.

"It's my son, Sipho. I was heavy with him the last time I saw you at the market."

"Is this him? He has grown so fast!" She clapped her hands in astonishment.

"Kids grow very fast these days," added my mother.

"And he's a splitting image of his father," the woman said.

"Oh! That one, he'd be very proud to hear that," my mother said, laughing.

The bus took off. There were many people talking at the same time. Some people were standing. They leaned on the iron bar that ran through the middle of the bus. They swerved this way and that, as the bus turned. Their voices were drowned by the roaring of the bus.

The bus crossed Matyana River, meandered through the Msengeni curves and went up "M" Street before arriving in Joza Township. "How come you are knocking off so early today, wife of my cousin?" I heard the woman ask. "Isn't it these silly white people?" my mother hissed back.

"Don't worry yourself about those," the woman said. "We'll throw them back to the sea within no time. Those houses are gonna be ours."

"Will that day ever come? I've lost hope now. I doubt even that Mandela is still alive. What kind of a man would refuse to come out of prison anyway?"

"Hey, wife of my cousin, I say hear me well," the woman said confidently. "We are gonna reclaim this land of our fathers. Even this street here is not gonna be called 'M' street any longer. It's gonna be Mandela Street," she said the words with emphasis.

"That's the day horses will grow horns," my mother said, holding my hand and getting ready to leave. We had reached our bus stop, known as *ezibhokhweni* – the place of goats. It was known as such because of the herd of goats bred by the family that lived near the bus stop.

As we got off the bus, my mother did not seem like she was in the mood for talking. She only answered whatever I said to her, and kept walking.

"Father will be happy to see us, isn't that so, Mama?"

"Yes, he'll be happy."

"Father loves us very much. Do you know that, Mama?"

"Yes, I know."

From a distance, we saw my father working in the garden. He used to say white people liked him because he had a "good hand". He didn't have a regular job, but white people called him every now and then to assist them with their gardening. Sometimes he would go to town and come back without having worked in any gardens. And when he did not get a job, sometimes he got angry. White people are ungrateful, he would say. Everyone knew that his plants grew fast – the plants that he ploughed for white people. Ours were not so lucky. Our soil at home was not fertile, that's why his plants didn't grow as fast at home as they did at the white man's place. But he always took good care of our garden, even though there was not much produce out of it.

"You must value the soil," my father would argue. "It's God's gift to humankind. We, ourselves, are made of this dust here." I didn't think we were made of dust because every time I scratched my skin, I saw blood, not dust. But I never questioned my father.

As we got closer to the house, he straightened himself and beat his hands together to shake the dust off. He took off his hat and wiped his brow with a handkerchief. He leaned against the spade and surveyed the garden. Then he left the spade and met us at the gate.

"How did it go?" he asked as we got into the yard.

"Fine," my mother responded.

"The doctor took out my tooth with a pliers," I reported.

"Did they extract it? Let me see," my father said, and I opened my mouth wide for him to see. "I see. Was it painful?"

"I didn't cry when the doctor took it out," I replied with pride.

"Very good. Now you are becoming a man."

Then he looked anxiously at my mother. "What's wrong?" he asked.

"There's nothing wrong, father of Sipho," my mother said.

"C'mon, I see something is not right. Did you fight with the doctor?"

"I've been fired."

"What?" My father frowned and his eyes seemed ready to pop out.

"It's like that, Father. It's long been coming. Since she divorced, she's been behaving strangely."

"But why?" He then turned to me: "Sipho, go to bed.

You need some rest." I went to the other room and lay on top of the blankets. I could hear everything they were saying. "What does she say she's firing you for?"

"For bringing my black son to work."

"She must be crazy. Did she want you to neglect your sick child and look after her spoilt brat?" My father was talking loudly.

"Mark is not a spoilt brat!" my mother objected.

"But it's so unfair. Doesn't she know that you are a mother too?"

"I should have first asked for permission to bring my child," my mother mumbled.

"But how do you know when your child will fall sick?" my father asked.

"I shouldn't have let Sipho play with Mark."

"Woman, don't take blame for this. Kids are kids. Black or white, they just play."

"I'm gonna miss Mark," my mother said.

"You've been unfairly dismissed and yet you still care about their child!"

"Mark is my child. He's the same age as Sipho here."

"Stop deceiving yourself. You'll never have a white child."

"I would've quit a long time ago. Mark is the only reason I stayed," my mother said. She seemed to be deep in thought as she spoke.

"You thought this boy was your child, and that's exactly the reason why my child grew up without his mother most of the time. You were busy taking care of that white woman's child." My father had amplified his voice.

"He's my child too. He is that big today because I breastfed him when he was an infant. His mother went back to work just a month after he was born," my mother's voice was beginning to sound shaky, "And we are separated, just like that, after six years!"

I must have fallen asleep while they were still talking. When I woke up, the air was filled with the smell of *amagwinya*, fat-cakes. My father was lying next to me, his nose buried in the family Bible. My mother was standing in front of the primus stove with a fork in her hand, preparing the *amagwinya*.

"Mama, I'm hungry," I announced.

"You'll eat now, son. I'm almost done." I knew "almost done" could mean anything. "When will you finish reading that?" I asked my father.

"You never finish reading a Bible, son. It should be our daily bread."

"How can a book become bread?" I was hungry at that very moment, hungry enough to eat the Bible if it were to become bread.

"What I mean is that we must consume it continuously through our living days."

"But I don't like the Bible stories."

"The Bible is the word of God. It is there to guide us at all times," he said.

"But the Bible stories are never as good as yours. The Bible hero gets killed whereas you and your brothers always win your fights. Just like in films."

Our conversation was interrupted by a knock at the door. Instinctively, I jumped to open the door. I removed the metal latch and the door swung open. I was engulfed by a shadow of blue. There in front of me was an enormous white man in a blue police uniform. I had seen him before. Everyone in the township knew him. Older boys used to run for cover at the sight of his yellow police van. It didn't matter that they were not involved in any unlawful activities. Their sin was being young men in a disorderly state.

I had never seen the horrendous policeman so close before. Now he was right in front of me. In my father's house. In our home. I still do not understand how he managed to walk through the door, because the man seemed bigger and taller than the door.

"*Ngubani lowo?*" my father shouted from the other room, asking who was there. The white man went past me.

"*Heyi, yiz' apha wena!*" He called on my father in a very demeaning manner. I understood very well that "*heyi*" was a very offensive and derogatory word to use. Now the policeman was referring to my father as "*heyi*". My father always regaled me with heroic stories of him and his three brothers. How no one could defeat them in stick-fighting. From the Great Fish River, across the Tyhume River and throughout the entire region of the Amathole Mountains, the brothers were respected warriors. No one could beat them, he had told me. The scars that criss-crossed his forehead were evidence of their might.

My father had been called outside by the policeman. He was following the policeman's orders. His manhood was diminishing right in front of me, my mother and the nosy onlookers. He didn't have his stick with him. The policeman had his gun with him. My father was there talking to the enormous policeman. And then I heard my mother's voice. My mother, the soft-spoken woman, sounded different. She was shouting. I had never heard her shout before. But that day she was shouting. Shouting at the white policeman. I was proud of my mother.

The door opened gently. It was my father, with my mother in tow.

"What are they saying, Tata?" I asked.

"They say I stole a car," he duly explained.

"When?" I am not sure whether I was asking when he had stolen the car or when the policeman said he had stolen it.

"Now."

"But you've been working here the whole day," I said with devastation.

"That's what I've been telling them. But they found the car outside our gate."

"What colour is it?" I asked, getting curious.

"It's red."

Red car, red car, you are outside my home.

How I wished the car could be given to my father if it was lost. He would learn how to drive it and would surely take good care of it. I once picked up a stray puppy and grew very fond of it. I named him Chomie because he became my friend. The same could happen to the car if it was lost. It was no big deal, I concluded.

The door swung open again. It was the stout policeman. "*Yiz' apha!*" he said, and my father didn't move an inch. I looked at my father and his face set in a defiant grimace. The policeman pointed at me with his fat finger.

"*Heyi, ndithetha nawe,*" he said, making it clear that he was talking to me and not to my father. I noticed for the first time that he had blue eyes. I never knew that white people could have blue eyes. Maybe with those eyes he couldn't tell that I was a child, I said to myself.

"*Heyi, ngumntwana lo.*" I felt so proud when my father said "*heyi*" to the dreaded policeman, telling him that I was only a child. The policeman fixed his gaze on me, and in the same way my father had done earlier, I got up and went outside with him.

"Who stole that car, is it your father?" he asked in Xhosa. I looked in the direction he was pointing, and there were many cars. There were many bystanders, too. I tried to respond, but my throat was dry and nothing audible came out of my mouth. He repeated the same words. I swallowed saliva and gave it one more try. I heard my hoarse and shaky voice saying, "I don't know." As soon as those words came out of my mouth, I felt a warm liquid trickling down my cheeks.

"Listen here, *boetie*, did your father steal that car?" The rhino in front of me persisted. He spoke slowly through clenched teeth, putting emphasis on each syllable. He touched the bulge at his waist, like a cowboy getting ready for a gunfight. I knew very well what police kept at their waists. The thought of violent death visited my young mind for the first time. My mother screamed that the policeman was about to kill me. My father shouted that the white pig dared to touch his son. I wet my khaki shorts.

Until that day, I had always looked up to my father. I knew my father was invincible. But at that moment I wondered what my father could do against such an enormous white man. My father was a small man, and his homemade rusty bayonet did not stand a chance against the white man's gun. Numerous guns. I had never seen so many cars around my home before. They were driven by the police. And police always had guns.

"You are not taking my son anywhere," my father kept shouting at the white man. "You rather kill me," he offered himself as a sacrifice.

The enormous white man in front of me bent to my height. I could smell his warm whiff. He was talking, but I couldn't hear anything any more. I was crying. And he beckoned me to go back into the house. My wet shorts stuck to my skin as I walked. My father was talking to the policeman. I wondered if the policeman was going to take my father's life as my father had offered. I didn't want to lose my father.

After what seemed like eternity, both my parents came back inside with undisguised fury across their faces. My mother was grumbling about disrespectful white men. My father couldn't believe that they would accuse him of being a car thief when he could not drive even a tractor. I wished my father had a car.

Red car, red car, how I long for you.

"Mama!" I called out to my mother.

"Yes, my dear little boy," she said, in English. She tried to force a smile as she turned to look at me. The phrase was from a nursery rhyme she had coined for me: "Oh my dear little baby; Oh my dear little boy." I would giggle and kick the air as she held me above her head and repeated the words. Those were just about the only English words familiar to me, even though I didn't know what they meant at the time.

"I hate white people." As soon as I said those words, my mother took a glance at my father. I also looked at my father. He took the blanket and covered his face. My mother drank water from a jug and hummed her favourite church hymn. I was disappointed that my comment had not been received with adulation.

There was another knock at the door. Gentler this time. It was another white man. He wore a white short-sleeved shirt. He had hair on his arms. He had a star outside his left chest-pocket. He had nicely trimmed black hair and was clean-shaven. He was handsome. If he was in a movie, he would definitely be playing the starring role. Handsome people don't deserve to be thugs!

He spoke in a tongue that I couldn't understand – presumably white people's tongue. My father responded without getting up. The white man said something to my mother also. My mother responded in a strange tongue. White people's tongue, I assumed. The white man turned to me. He pulled my cheek gently with his two fingers and said a familiar sound. The same sound that my mother would make when she saw a cute baby. He made a gesture like a goodbye. I lifted my right hand and waved at the handsome white man. He was smiling as he opened the door to leave. That was the last I saw of him. And the last time I saw a white man in our house.

"Oh! My fat-cakes have burned!" my mother cried, making a dash towards the primus stove. She switched it off. And only then was I conscious of the smell and the smoke that filled the house. I took off my wet khaki shorts and got into bed next to my father.

"What did the white man say, Tata?" I asked.

"You mean the one with a white shirt?"

"Yes, that one who did not yell."

"It was all a mistake," my father said without enthusiasm. With my eyes, I implored him to explain more. He then told me that the white man that came last had seen and chased the thief all the way from Port Elizabeth, but he had gotten away. He knew what the culprit looked like. And that it wasn't my father.

Bhontsi's Toe

◆

BHONTSI HAS GOT A big toe.

We call it the magic toe. It has done miracles for the team. It helps him to kick the ball very hard. He plays as a defender most of the time, but he scores the most goals. He kicks the ball from one side of the field and scores in the other. He is our best player.

Bhontsi plays with bare feet.

His toe is too big to be contained in shoes. He does not have shoes. It is not to his liking that he does not have any shoes. He has no parents to buy shoes for him. He does not know who his father is. He was told that his father came to Grahamstown with a construction company. The workers lived in tents and left after finishing the road that they were building. Bhontsi's mother did not know where to find the man who had made her heavy with child. So Bhontsi was born a fatherless child.

Bhontsi's mother died.

She suffered from a heart disease. Bhontsi took turns with his two sisters to take their mother to the local clinic. They would get tablets from the nurses to help her live. But the tablets could not save her life forever. She died. Bhontsi now lives with his elder sisters. His sisters also do not have regular jobs. Sometimes they wash clothes and clean houses for rich families in the township. The families of teachers, nurses and police live comfortable lives; they have TVs in their homes and eat rice every day. They send other people's children to work for them. They can afford to give small change to other people. Bhontsi's sisters receive a "thank you" from the people they work for. When they get money, they buy food for themselves and Bhontsi to eat. Bhontsi sometimes goes for days on an empty stomach; he told me that the other day when I shared my food with him.

Bhontsi is a grown man now.

He is only twelve, just a year older than me. He looks after himself, the way grown-up men are wont to do, that's what he said to me the other day. Sometimes he works and then he buys food for himself with the "thank you" he receives from people. He usually goes to the police barracks. His sisters play with their male friends in the barracks. They sometimes sleep there. Their male friends are police.

Police shoot people.

People kill the police. They make the police wear tyres like necklaces and set them alight. Sometimes they throw bottles filled with petrol and sand into police houses. Sometimes the *impimpis* are also burned to death by the people. The *impimpis* tell police where to find the people called terrorists. The people called terrorists kill other people, the *impimpis* say. The soldiers want to kill terrorists, too. I have seen soldiers, they are brown, and I have seen police too, they are blue, but I do not know the colour of the terrorist.

My father says the war was started by the police and the soldiers, who are trying to kill the terrorists. The *impimpis* and other people get hit the way you hit the branch of a tree trying to hit a bird sitting on it. He says there are no terrorists. The people killed by the soldiers and police are comrades fighting for our liberation. I don't know what they want to liberate us from. But I've seen the lifeless body of a comrade, lying still in a pool of thick blood. He was shot by the police, they say.

I don't want my father to die.

I asked my father if he was a comrade. "You, you have a big mouth," he said. I went to my mother in the kitchen and said to her, "Mother, do you think father is a comrade?" She turned and slapped me with a wet dishcloth: "You are going to be an *impimpi*, this curious little thing!"

I don't want to be an *impimpi*. I don't want to be a comrade, either. I just want to be a child. I want to play soccer and be happy every day.

The police are friendly to Bhontsi.

Sometimes they send him to the shops. The other times they tell him to bring their girls. Bhontsi says one of them gave him a real gun to hold the other day. Bhontsi says the real gun was heavy in his hand. It made his hand shake and there were drumbeats in his chest. Bhontsi does not want to hold a real gun again. He just wants to get money to buy food. The police give him food sometimes. On other occasions, they give him money. When he comes back from the shop with small change, they say, "Keep the change, *my laaitie*." He gets a lot of money that way.

He collected enough "thank you" money to buy himself a pair of black Idler shoes. The front of the shoes had a square shape like the nose of a cow.

Bhontsi's shoes got a big hole.

It was barely a week after he bought himself the new shoes, and other children were already making fun of Bhontsi. They said he didn't know how to walk with shoes. He walked like a castrated monkey, they said. I didn't like what they were saying about Bhontsi. "These shoes are eating me, sonny," he said.

"Why don't you stop wearing them?" I asked.

"You guys are gonna laugh at me."

"I won't, sonny. I promise."

"Others will laugh. And you will also laugh when they laugh. They laugh when I don't have shoes. They also laugh when I have the shoes. What do they want?" Bhontsi asked. He sounded devastated. I wanted to console him.

"Don't worry, sonny. We'll tell them to go to hell."

Bhontsi wears size six. He wears the same size as my eldest sister who goes to the big schools. It was strange to see Bhontsi in shoes, but I was glad that he looked like other children. But soon his toe was peeping through as if watching and listening to everything that was happening outside. Bhontsi says he does not understand how the hole was opened. He only felt fresh air on his toe and that's when he realised that there was a hole in his shoe.

Bhontsi does not wear shoes any more.

He's got the toughest feet around. Some say he's got crocodile feet. They are wrong. Crocodiles don't play soccer. Bhontsi is good at soccer. They also don't walk long distances as Bhontsi does. The police send Bhontsi to faraway places. Sometimes they ask him to buy bread for them. Sometimes he buys liquor from the tavern. Sometimes they send him to a faraway place, where he buys the green stuff for the police. He knows how to hide the green stuff from the other police. He never puts it in his pockets because his pockets have holes. He folds his pants and puts the green stuff in there. The police love the green stuff. It makes them happy. They laugh loud and even shoot in the air after smoking it.

Bhontsi is not available to play today.

I saw him going to the police barracks this morning. He was clad in his usual maroon pants and brown T-shirt. These clothes had been on Bhontsi's body for a very long time. Some say he is a cow because he never changes his colours. The T-shirt is now full of holes. There are more holes than there is a T-shirt. He was carrying plastic bags, full of many nice things. He was taking the nice things to the barracks.

I asked him to come with us to the match. But he said he was unable to join us. He said he was visiting the barracks with his two sisters and their male friends.

"It's end of the month, sonny," he said. "The police got paid yesterday and I'm gonna get lots of tips today."

"Please drop those things and come back, sonny. You'll go after the match," I pleaded with him.

"I can't, sonny. Today is very busy. I have to burn the meat and do many things."

He explained that the police were very generous when they got drunk. They would send him to the tavern to get more beer. Every trip would be worth a tip. They would also put meat on burning coals. The police didn't know how to make fire. Bhontsi would prepare everything for them. They would leave him with the meat. He would take meat from the *braai* stand while they were busy cuddling his sisters. I salivated at the mere mention of burned meat. I would have loved to taste that meat. But there was a match to play. And Bhontsi told me that it was his job to assist the lazy cops.

"Job is job, sonny!" he said. Bhontsi left school at Standard One, after the death of his mother. I don't know when he learned to speak the white man's language. But that's what he said. And then he went to the barracks.

We need Bhontsi's magic toe to score for us.

The score now is 8–5 and we are leading. I have scored three of the eight goals. The game will end if we score two more goals. I don't want to score. There will be another fight if the game ends now. The other boys will beat me because I scored. They always want to fight after the end of a game, especially when they lose. Bhontsi is not here to fight for us. His hands are as tough as his feet. All the other boys are scared of him. I have never seen Bhontsi beating anyone. They are just scared of him. They are scared of his toe. They say with those big feet he could kick a pig to death. I still hope that Bhontsi will come and join us.

Unexpected guests come.

A convoy of Hippos, Casspirs and other armoured vehicles emerge from behind the police barracks. Soldiers wearing brown clothes and helmets appear atop the vehicles. They are carrying automatic rifles like they are carrying brooms. The rifles are pointed towards the sky. We stop playing. We stand frozen. No one says anything. All of us are looking in the direction of the soldiers. Three Casspirs come towards us while the rest of the convoy drives through the township. The terror of last night is back to haunt me even though the sun is piercing the soil.

I slept under the bed last night.

My mother saw a security searchlight beaming through our windows. She peeped through the keyhole and saw a convoy of armoured vehicles coming towards the township. She turned to my father and said, "It's a raid!" My mother's eyes were large. My father jumped up and also took a look through the keyhole. He then turned to my mother and said, "Let's hide the children!"

Our house is the first one in the township. If the soldiers wanted to destroy all the people in the township, they would start with our family. We were told to hide under the bed, my sister and I. My mother poured a bucket of water into a plastic washing basin. She dipped my shirt into the water and gave it to me. She did the same for my sister.

We heard the big engines roaring past.

There was no knock at our door. There was no smell of tear-gas. There were no gunshots. My mother said we should stay under the bed. We did not know when the soldiers would come back. We stayed there until I fell asleep. When I woke up in the morning, I was sneezing endlessly. I looked in the mirror. The boy in the mirror had bloodshot eyes. His face looked pale and dry. There was grey cat fur and spiderwebs on my clothes. I dusted them and raised a lot of dust. My mother said I must wash myself.

Bhontsi is not afraid of the soldiers.

I told him about the raid that we survived last night. He explained that that was not a raid, but a patrol. He said that Botha had declared a state of emergency.

"What's an emergency?" I asked.

"It means the soldiers are looking for terrorists at night."

"And they do that by driving around in Casspirs?" I asked.

"That's why you guys can no longer walk in the streets at night. You'll be shot because the soldiers will think you are the terrorists," Bhontsi had explained expertly.

But now the soldiers are coming to us in the soccer field.

There is no bed to hide under. There are no parents to protect us. Even Bhontsi is not here. We are just standing here, not knowing what to do. If we run, they will shoot us. If we stay, they will torture us.

The Casspirs stop just outside the soccer field. The soldiers leave their rifles with their colleagues in the vehicles. They say something in a strange language. Miki lifts his hand and then steps forward. He says something that I do not understand. Miki knows how to speak many languages. He goes to the school for Coloured children where they learn to speak many languages.

Miki then turns to us: "Gents, they are not gonna shoot us. They just want to play." Miki looks at the soldiers. They nod and say something in their language. Miki tells us that they speak Afrikaans, and that he is going to interpret for us. Miki learns Afrikaans at school and that's the language he uses when he speaks to his Coloured friends.

"They are not the real soldiers. They are school children just like us. But they have been taken into the military. They will finish their training soon and go to university to become newspaper men." I don't trust much of what Miki is saying about the soldiers not being real soldiers. They are wearing real uniforms, they ride real Casspirs, and they are carrying real guns. But the prospect of playing with white people is too enticing for me to object.

We play soccer with the soldiers who are not really soldiers.

They form one team. And we form the other. I don't know how many players there are in the field. There is no referee. We just play, not caring about soccer rules. We dribble past the soldiers. They don't have skills, these soldiers. Miki calls them *skop en jaag*, because they just kick the ball and run after it. They laugh at Miki's joke. They kick us with their army boots when they try to take the ball from us. We don't mind because we play fancy tricks on them and they keep chasing our shadows. They barely touch the ball. I even put the ball through one's legs. He turns hurriedly, trying to catch up with me. I put the ball through his legs again. Miki bursts out laughing. The soldier kicks him gently on the buttocks. Two more Casspirs arrive. When some of the soldiers get tired, they go out the field and others come and play. Those that are resting sit and drink beer. Some smoke the green stuff. I can smell it. The soldiers are happy.

The clouds have gathered.

The sky has now turned grey. There is fresh air, smelling of rain. We know the rain will fall in torrents soon. But the game is just too nice to abandon. Bhontsi would have enjoyed the game. I'm gonna tell him all about it. I know he would say, "*Eish!* I wish I was there, sonny."

"I told you to come with me. You see now, we play with white people, just like the professionals on TV," I would tell him and he would envy us.

The ball is becoming harder. I don't mind the hardness of the ball because I have soccer boots. I am the only one with soccer boots in our team. Other boys play with bare feet, *tekkies* or sometimes with their school shoes. My father picked up the boots in one of the white people's gardens. White people are lucky; their gardens even grow soccer boots. But now it is raining. And we have to stop playing when it is raining.

Bhongo says the rain is just passing. I think it is passing too. The soldiers are also enjoying themselves. No one wants to stop playing.

The rain is falling hard.

At first we think it is gonna stop. But then it continues and rains harder than before. We take off our shirts and play with bare chests. The rain hits directly on our bodies. We enjoy the feeling of the rain on our naked skins. If Bhontsi was here, he would have enjoyed this game. He likes walking around half-naked. Bhontsi's body has got big muscles and a thick skin. He can walk around with a bare chest on a cold day and never get sick. The other boys say he's got rhino skin. I know that the other reason Bhontsi likes not wearing clothes is because his clothes are always torn.

But Bhontsi is not here. We are playing in the rain. My underpants are becoming wet. My mother will be angry when I get home drenched in water. The soldiers scurry away. They board their Casspirs and leave in haste. We go to the old cars on the open field nearby. The Casspirs drive off.

We sit inside the two cars.

I take the driver's seat. Bhongo leaves the other car

because it does not have a steering wheel. He tells me to move over because he is the driver. He is only doing this because Bhontsi is not here. Bhontsi wouldn't let anyone treat me like that. He always protects me. I vacate the space and sit next to Miki in the back seat. Bhongo starts turning the steering wheel this way and that. He makes the sound of a moving car with his mouth. He always has wild visions of himself as a truck driver. The car has got no windows. It doesn't have doors either. But it provides nice shelter from the rain. It is raining heavily. We don't see where the Casspirs went. We cannot see the goal posts. We cannot see the barracks. I wonder what if the rain continues until tomorrow.

It stops raining as suddenly as it had started. Water is dripping down the sides of our shelter. Small ponds of brown water form on the ground. Bhongo stands in the car and pees into the water. Other boys follow suit. There is a contest of who can pee furthest. I don't join the peeing game. The other boys will make fun of me just like last time. Bhongo has got hair around his pubic area. It is new hair, soft and shiny. He said I was still a child because I didn't have any hair on my pubis. He caught a butterfly and smeared its powdery wings on my pubic area. He said that would help me grow the hair. But still the hair hasn't grown.

A flock of swallows emerges from the side of the sky where the sun rises.

They flap their wings and perform a spectacular display of acrobatics in the sky. They all look black. I wonder if the swallows can distinguish their friends and relatives when they all look the same. If I were a swallow, I would hate to mistake someone like Bhongo for my relative. There must be good swallows and bad swallows.

Bhongo takes out his sling.

We all remember to retrieve our slings, which we keep hidden in the two cars. The police arrest and shoot boys with slings. The slings are said to be dangerous weapons. That's why we have to hide our slings. We collect pebbles from the ground and try to shoot at the swallows. We don't come anywhere close to hitting any. The swallows fly too fast and too high in the sky.

"There's the line of boobs!" Miki says. We all look in the direction he is pointing. "What is a line of boobs?" Bhongo asks.

"Look at the horizon, you see those beautiful colours?"

"Wow! It's so beautiful," I say.

"Check the semblance of colours. It's like magic." The colours appear as if they have been arranged by an artist. They start in the sky and disappear on the edge of the horizon.

"Let's go see," Miki says. I am about to object, but all other boys are already running towards the rainbow. I join them and we race each other down the open field and towards the AmaZion Dam where the rainbow seems to fall. We all know that no one dares get into the dam unless you are going there with your church. The people of Zion church are baptised here. It makes them stronger because the underwater people live in AmaZion Dam. Sometimes the underwater people call people to the underworld and the families must not cry because when they come back, they will be the best healers. They will be given the strength and the wisdom of the people of the underworld to help us on earth. Most of the time, people cry and the swallowed people never come back alive.

The rainbow falls onto the other side of the road.

We cross the road only to find another small stream. The stream is surrounded by reeds. We can see the fading colours of the rainbow hanging spectacularly above the stream. Bhongo takes out his sling and tries to hit through the rainbow with a pebble. The pebble causes ripples in the water. Miki also takes out his sling and aims it at the water. His pebble causes bigger ripples than Bhongo's. More slings are drawn out. More pebbles hit the water. Now we have a contest to see who will cause the biggest ripples in the water.

A duck comes out of a corner behind the reeds.

It quacks and opens big ripples as it glides on the water. Two ducklings appear behind it. They are yellowish with fine dots on the wings. They squeak constantly as they battle to catch up with their mother. The mother quacks once to every three squeaks made by the little birds. The sound of the ducks has some melody to it.

"Do you know that a duck works hard to remain floating?" Miki asks. We all look at him in astonishment.

"This one is crazy. Don't you know that it's floating because it's in the nature of ducks to float?" Bhongo replies.

"But it works hard to keep afloat. If you were to see its feet you'd understand that it's paddling very hard, even though it appears effortless on the surface."

"You know what, I have a better use for this bird." So says Bhongo, pulling on his sling. He aims, releases the sling and the pebble hits very close to the duck, causing more ripples. There are more squeaks. Six more ducklings appear and follow the direction of the mother and the other two.

"No, don't kill the duck. What will happen to its ducklings?" I ask.

"Go to hell! I want that meat," Bhongo says as he pulls the sling again.

"Please don't," Miki intervenes. Bhongo misses by an inch and the duck flies away.

"We will kill its children, then," declares Bhongo and

pulls the sling.

"Bhongo, please don't do this!" Miki says, but it's too late. Bhongo releases the sling and the pebble hits a duckling. The duckling does not squeak. Its lifeless body just floats on the water. The rest of the ducklings swim helter-skelter, going to all directions. Their mother is hovering in the sky above the stream. She keeps quacking over our heads. Bhongo jumps and throws his hands in the sky to celebrate the hit. The other boys congratulate him. If Bhontsi was here, he would stop Bhongo from killing the innocent birds. But no one among us has the courage to stop Bhongo. Instead, other boys join him. More pebbles hit the water. There is less squeaking. And there are more celebrations as more lifeless bodies float.

"I am not gonna sit through this," Miki says and turns away. The other boys ignore him. They are occupied with their killing game. I sneak off and follow Miki, constantly glancing behind me to watch the other boys. We could be the next targets!

Our shadows are taller than us.

I have a curfew at home. Only Bhontsi knows about this. The other boys would laugh at me if they were to know. My father always tells me that when I am playing with my friends, I must look at my shadow, and if the shadow is taller than me, then the sun is about to set; and I must not be playing outside when the sun sets. Now the sun is about to set. Miki and I are walking home. We keep glancing behind us. The other boys are standing in a single file taking turns to shoot at the ducklings. Occasionally they give each other high-fives, and I know that another life is lost.

We see a small circle of people ahead of us.

There are white people, too. They are looking anxiously at something on the ground. They are wearing blue uniforms. There are two yellow vans standing nearby.

"It's the cops!" Miki announces. We hide our slings in our pockets. One of the white policemen is standing over black ashes on the ground. He is not wearing any uniform. He is taking pictures with a camera. In the middle of the circle are charred remains of a burned tyre. Someone has been necklaced!

There is dull smoke still rising. The smell of a burned tyre hangs in the air. As we walk past, I see a piece of cloth. It is maroon in colour. There is a bit of human organ showing underneath it. I start quivering. I grab Miki's hand and hold it tightly.

"That is Bhontsi's toe," Miki whispers to my ear. I take another look. The small piece of cloth does look like the pants that Bhontsi was wearing this morning. It is lying in the ashes. The ashes are Bhontsi's body. The rhino skin has been reduced into ashes. But Bhontsi's toe did not get burned. We walk briskly ahead. I don't want to look again.

Hunger

◆

MY STOMACH GROWLED AGAIN.

I turned to face the other side. I lay in a foetal position, pulling my knees up to my torso to suppress the pangs of hunger. They subsided for a while. Then there was a heavy traffic of wind-balls running up and down my stomach. I pressed my hand against my abdomen and released wind. The air filled with the smell of rotten eggs. I felt empty, nauseous and hungrier than before. I had performed this exercise throughout the night.

A dove cooed from the top of the big gum tree. It had a nest there and would coo every morning until everybody woke up. I opened my eyes. There was a small light coming through the slit in the curtain. I pushed the curtain to the side. The tips of cattle horns were showing above the walls of the kraal. A single cloud hung spectacularly above the mountains on the horizon. There was no threat of rain.

There came a knock at the door.

"Who is that?" my grandmother shouted from the other room.

"It's Nomatse, Grandma," the visitor responded.

"Nomatse! What is a squirrel doing in our homestead so early in the morning?" Grandmother wondered.

"I am here to ask for cow dung, Grandma," Nomatse said.

"Cow dung so early in the morning!" Grandmother exclaimed.

"Yes, Grandma, I thought I should come early so I

would get it fresh."

"You are a squirrel and you want fresh cow dung early in the morning?" Grandmother tried to make sense of what Nomatse was saying.

"Eh, Grandma," I intervened. "Nomatse is the daughter of uncle Mpangele from the Bheles." I could tell that my grandmother did not understand that "Nomatse" was actually the name of the girl, and not a squirrel as the name suggested.

"Oh, Mpangele. The one with the eyes of a guinea fowl?"

"Yes, uncle Mpangele, Grandma."

"Why didn't she say so? Alright, go ahead, child. Get yourself some cow dung."

"Thank you, Grandma," Nomatse said and proceeded to the kraal. This was her routine. She woke up very early on Fridays and went to those homesteads that still had cattle in their kraals. The droughts had left many kraals in the village bare.

My grandmother had consultations with the Creator every night before going to bed, begging him to spare the lives of the three cows, two calves and one bull that we still had in our kraal until I was old enough to marry. She was convinced that I would marry Nonqaba, her friend's granddaughter, who was the lead singer in the church choir. Pity Nonqoba's appearance didn't match her voice. Besides, I only had eyes for Nonzwakazi, a third-year student at the University of Fort Hare, just like me. Nonzwakazi had gone home to Mqanduli after the campus closed down two weeks ago due to the raging student protests against the exorbitant and continually escalating fees.

My back was itchy. I reached for the area and tried to scratch it. I could feel the prints of the grass-mat with the tips of my fingers. I got up and stretched myself. There was a bulge in my shorts. I had to take a leak to rid myself of the hardness. A cold breeze hit my half-naked body as I stepped outside. I peed against the wall of the kraal. Nomatse was so engrossed in her job of collecting cow dung that she didn't even notice me. Her bucket was full, but she kept piling up the dung with her now green hands. She had to get enough to smear on the floor of her entire homestead.

The cattle went about their business as usual, munching yesterday's grass, which they kept in their mouths. They occasionally swished their tails in an effort to purge away the flies that used their backsides as landing strips. Their skeletal frames bore testament to the devastating drought. The cows looked deformed, with their bloated udders hanging under their scrawny bodies. The calves mooed from the small enclosure, eager to join their parents in the kraal and have their breakfast. What they did not seem to understand is that human beings were in charge, and had to milk the cows before allowing the calves to feed from what little was left.

I went back to the house, wiped my face clean and changed into my tracksuit and running shoes. "Are you going to school again today, Grandson?" asked my grandmother.

"Yes, Grandma. I'll give it a try once more."

"Tell them that if they don't sort this matter out today, I'll go there myself," she threatened.

"Yes, Grandma. I will tell them." My grandmother inhabited a world where delusionary visions superseded logical reasoning. She saw herself as an invincible superwoman who could solve anything and everything on the surface of the earth. She had lived in Mavuso village all her life, but had never set a foot on the premises of the

University of Fort Hare, which was separated from the village by a single hill. That same person thought she could sort out my money problems with the University, where throngs of students had to jostle for resources.

The set-up in the Dean of Students' office was the same as on all my previous visits. The door was wide open. Kate, the volunteer administrator from Denmark, was busy typing emails and chewing gum simultaneously. Occasionally, she would jot some notes in her ever-present journal. She was slim and of average height. Her long brown hair lay in strands over her shoulders. She had a warm personality, this Kate, always eager to have a conversation. She had previously told me that she had come to South Africa to do in-service training for her Masters Degree in Rural Development. Mr Kensington saw it fit that she should spend most of her time behind a computer in the air-conditioned office.

She constantly blew gum, making bubbles and deflating them. I cleared my throat, in an attempt to get her attention. She lifted her eyes and a smile spread across her face.

"Hey, Mr Mayekiso. Good to see you again," she said, broadening the smile and flashing nicotine-tinged teeth.

"Hi, I hope I'm not disturbing. Is the Dean in today?"

"He's not here yet. But you can take a seat if you don't mind waiting," she said, pointing at the waiting area across the room. There were three sofas and a coffee table. The table was littered with magazines and University prospectuses. The door to the Dean's office was closed. Kate continued typing and reading emails. She occasionally squinted her eyes to focus. Her lips would move as if she was having a silent conversation with the computer screen in front of her. A smile spread across her face.

"I wish I could be the one putting that smile on your face," I remarked.

"Sorry, I didn't get that. What did you say?" she asked, lifting her head to look at me. "The smile," I repeated, "I wish I could be the one putting it on your face." I had been gathering courage to say something like this to her for a very long time.

"Oh, that," she chuckled. "I didn't notice that I was smiling. It's this message from this guy," she said, giggling helplessly.

"Your boyfriend must be a fun kind of guy, heh?" I said.

"You got that wrong, actually. This guy is just a pervert that I 'met' online. He does make me laugh though, that much is true," she said, still with a wide grin. "So, Mr Mayekiso," she went on, a bit more hesitant, "where are you from, I mean, you come here quite often even though the campus has been shut down?"

"Please call me Sipho. I'm from Grahamstown."

"That's about…" she took a pocket-book from her desk. The book had *A Rough Guide to the Eastern Cape* written on the cover, and she paged through it hurriedly.

"That's about a hundred kilometres from here, isn't it?" she asked.

"Yes, it is." I was not so sure about the distance, but what I knew was that I had travelled it often enough to know that I was R30 poorer after every trip.

"Gosh! How do you manage to travel from there every week? They should sort this matter out already."

"I hope they do." There was no point in prolonging the story, bringing up all the issues of me staying with my grandmother, who lived in a nearby village.

"So, you are Kosa?" she asked.

"Not Kosa. I am Xhosa. X–x–x–. Say it," I instructed.

"That sounds nice. C–c–c–. Cosa," she said, and we both burst into uproarious laughter at her absurd effort. "C'mon, teach me how to say it," she said, still laughing.

"I think we'll need more time for these lessons – outside office hours, of course."

"Sure, I have all the time in the world. I always wanted to learn the language anyway," she said, to my delight.

"So, where are you staying?

"I'm staying at Elukhanyisweni Residence," she said. Elukhanyisweni, the Place of Light, was the most glamorous student residence on campus. Only postgraduates stayed there. Although the campus was closed down, there were still postgraduate students around, as many of them worked on campus.

"And how are you finding South Africa so far?" I asked.

"I like it here but I, I kinda haven't travelled much, you know. There are a few places that I wanna see but I'm scared of crime," she said, frowning.

"C'mon, it's not that bad. Especially if you travel with a local," the patriot in me prodded, inspired by the prospect of becoming Kate's personal guide.

"Can you travel with me, then? I want to go to Hogsback. Have you ever been there?" she asked.

"I go there all the time," I said. In actual fact, that was the truth in reverse. I had never been to Hogsback before, but I had heard about it, what it looked like and what tourists enjoyed there the most. "It's a nice place, that," I decided to add.

"Are you going with me tomorrow, then?" I could see the sparkle in her eyes as she asked the question.

"For sure. No problem," I said without thinking.

"But are you gonna travel to Grahamstown today and come back in the morning?"

"No. Actually, I can crash at a friend's place tonight."

"Great, so please meet me at the Residence at five tomorrow morning. I'd like us to get there before sunrise," she said, scribbling her room number on a piece of paper.

She gave me the piece of paper and that was the moment I heard the shuffling of Mr Kensington's feet. He came in as I turned to go back to the sofa in the waiting area. He was a very short man and his shiny bald patch glittered under the office light. He was carrying a briefcase in one hand, and a lunch box in the other.

"Young man, I see you've made yourself comfortable in my office," he said. I had gotten used to his way of greeting.

"Good morning, Sir," I said, going back to the sofa. Mr Kensington wore a khaki safari suit. He had thick glasses and a pipe hung below his bushy moustache. He put the briefcase on the floor and took a bunch of keys from his pocket. He dropped the keys as he was about to open the door to his office. He bent down to pick them up, revealing the outline of his buttocks. Seeing that he was struggling, I picked up the keys for him.

"Thank you, young man," he said, opening the door to his office. Kate got up, a diary in hand, and strutted towards her boss's office. She closed the door behind her, but I could hear whispering.

"Why did you allow him to wait for me?" I heard Mr Kensington ask. Kate replied, but I couldn't hear what she was saying because she had muffled her voice. When she re-emerged, she flashed a bleak smile.

"He'll see you in a minute," she said, trying to hide her frustration.

"Thanks," I said. After a while, her phone rang. She had a short conversation with the caller and after putting down the handset, she told me that Mr Kensington was ready for me.

"Take a seat, young man," he said, ushering me to one of the two chairs in front of his desk.

"What did you say you wanted again?" asked Mr Kensington, opening a file in front of him. Inside it were my previous letters to the University, my academic transcripts and my grandmother's old-age grant certificate.

"All I want is an opportunity to pursue my studies and finish my degree, Sir," I said.

"Boy, you expect us to pay for your tuition, accommodation and feed you. Everything!" He threw his hands in the air.

"I have nowhere else to go, Sir."

"How did you survive the past two years? Can't your parents pay for your registration at least?" he asked.

"My parents are not alive, Sir. My father died last year. He's the one who used to assist me with his pension money," I explained.

"So, you are an orphan?"

"No, Sir. I am not an orphan."

"Didn't you just say your parents are not alive?"

"That does not make me an orphan, Sir."

"Boy, you are not making any logical sense. Don't waste my time here."

"Sir, I would think of an orphan as someone who has no one, and I am not that. You don't find that even among the cattle, Sir. If a cow dies, leaving a calf, the calf becomes part of a herd, a community of cattle. It will never be alone. It is the case with our culture as well."

"That's an interesting take," he said, nodding gently and taking a drag from his pipe. "So, Mr Philosopher, where is your community of cattle then? Who do you have now to belong to?" As he spoke, smoke poured out of his mouth and nose like the chimney of a coal train.

"I have my grandmother who is a pensioner, Sir," I said. He shook his head and paged through a thick book in front of him.

"Your academic record is not bad. Maybe we should see you on Monday. I'm meeting with the Registrar to discuss cases like yours. There are many students who are facing similar problems. We'll be starting with the screening process next week."

"That would be wonderful, Sir," I said.

"Don't come too early on Monday. We can only see you after twelve, okay?"

"Yes, Sir. I'll be here after midday on Monday."

I left the campus in high spirits that day. I had been trying to secure a meeting with the management ever since the University opened some six weeks ago.

"How did it go at school today, Grandson?" Grandmother asked on my return, before I could even sit down.

"All is well, Grandma. They finally agreed to meet with me on Monday."

"That is wonderful news. What time are you meeting them on Monday?"

"They said I should be there at midday," I explained.

"Who is they, son? You keep saying 'they, they, they'. Are you talking about cattle that say moo-moo-moo, or you are talking about people with names?"

Grandmother barely ever left the house, let alone the village, except on payday when she went to receive her old-age grant in town. It was highly unlikely that she would know the Dean. I didn't understand why she bothered asking.

"You wouldn't know them, Grandma. I spoke to Mr Kensington, the Dean of Students. We will be in a meeting with Mr Mzila, the Registrar, who is the highest authority on this matter," I explained.

"Mzila," she said. "That is one of us, isn't he?"

"Yes, he's a black man in charge of big issues at University, Grandma."

"I see. They better let you study, child of my child," she said with finality.

I woke up early the following morning and left for campus. Kate was already waiting in her green VW Beetle, which had seen far too many years. She gave me a hug, the first I got from a white woman. And it was just like any other hug.

The Beetle left the campus, heading in the direction of Kingwilliamstown. It took a left turn towards Hogsback, roaring all the way as it meandered through the mountains and gorges. We approached from the west, with the sun still hiding behind the hog's back-shaped mountain before us. The scenery was almost devoid of human beings.

"This is splendid!" Kate screamed with excitement.

"Yes, it's great," I said, not sure what she was referring to exactly.

"Look at the clouds," she said, pointing to the clouds that hung above the mountain. "They are orange. I've never seen anything like this before."

We parked next to a stable with horses. There was a group of tourists *braai*-ing meat across from us. My nose followed the trail of barbecue like a starved dog.

"Let's go up the mountain," Kate said, opening the boot of her car. She took out her backpack, which contained, among the noticeable items, bottled water, a camera, sun-block cream, a pack of Camel cigarettes, a cigarette lighter, her journal and a pen. As we stood at the foot of the mountain, I thought about the journey ahead. A small footpath snaked up the mountain. My body shivered as soon as the image of a snake came to mind. I looked around my feet, just to make sure that there was no crawling reptile nearby.

"Are you gonna walk up that mountain?" I asked, with a bit of trepidation.

"We are gonna go up the mountain. We can take a horse trail, if you want. In fact, let's check if there are any horses available," she said, and I made a silent prayer for the unavailability of horses.

"We've only got one horse available at the moment, Ma'am. You may have to wait two hours or so to get another one," the enormous receptionist said.

"No, it's okay. Take the one that's available. I'll walk beside you," I said, protecting my dignity. I had never been on horseback before and I was not interested in learning how to ride in the presence of Kate.

"Are you sure?" Kate asked.

"I'm a runner, remember. Just ride that one," I said.

"That's so gentlemanly of you. But I'll give you a chance to ride when you get tired of walking," Kate offered.

We went up the mountain, Kate on horseback while I walked beside the horse. She could be fascinated by anything, this Kate. She would shout "Splendid!" at just about everything she came across. The weather, the vegetation, the horse, the rabbits and antelopes that dashed away as soon as they saw us, even the pink buttocks of the baboon that startled us as it climbed up an adjacent cliff – all were splendid! I began to doubt if the word had any meaning to her any more.

When we finally got to the top of the mountain, she dished out more "splendids". The scenery was splendid, the blue sky was splendid, and even the air was splendid. And she never forgot to make journal entries.

"Thank you, boo-boo," she said, kissing the horse's mane.

"I wish I could be a horse," I ventured, sitting down on a big stone.

"What?" she said.

"I said, I wish I could be a horse," I repeated. She smiled and got off the horse's back. "You mean to get the kiss, or the ride?"

"Maybe both," I said, matter-of-factly.

"You are crazy!" She kissed me on the cheek. "You ain't getting the ride, though," she said, taking the pack of cigarettes out her backpack. She offered me a cigarette and I took it. She shielded against the wind and lit her cigarette, before bringing the flame to me. Having the flame next to my face was not the most comfortable thing, but I tried to puff so the cigarette caught alight. I sneezed immediately and coughed uncontrollably.

"You don't smoke, do you?" she asked.

"No!" I shook my head, still coughing.

"Why didn't you say so?" she asked.

"I thought you'd say it's rude," I said, giving the cigarette back to her. She killed it, and then smoked hers.

"What else didn't you tell me about you?" she asked.

"That the other reason I went to the Dean's office so often was you."

"What about me?" she asked.

"I like you. I wanted to see you every day."

"Why didn't you just say so?" she said, smiling. She threw the cigarette stub away.

"I didn't have courage, I guess."

"What if I say I like you too?" she said, looking straight into my eyes. That warranted no verbal response. I kissed her pink lips. Her mouth smelled like ashtray. Our tongues wrestled each other. My south pole pointed north. Only the mountain, the trees and the horse were witness to this unfolding miracle.

I fell in love with the Hogsback Mountain that day. We went up as strangers, Kate and I, she riding on horseback and me walking besides the horse, like a slave. And we came back as lovers. We walked hand in hand as we went down the mountain, with Kate leading the horse behind us by its harness. Kate was not the most beautiful woman I had ever been with, but I was sure to earn respect among my fellow villagers for "eating white bread". We were two years into a democratic South Africa, but no man in Mavuso village had been able to advance the idealism of a rainbow nation by having a white woman lift her dress for him.

She took a picnic basket from the car. In it were apples, bananas, a bottle of Coke and bottled water. The snack of bananas and apples left my stomach an empty vessel. I wanted bread. But that would have been too much to ask from a new girlfriend.

"I like the texture of your hair," Kate said, brushing my hair with her hand. "Why don't you get the locks?" she asked.

"You want me to get dreadlocks?"

"For sure!" she said, squealing with excitement. "I find African guys with locks extremely sexy," she explained.

"I won't cut my hair again. I'll let it grow and form the locks," I said, even though I had no intention of growing dreadlocks. My grandmother wouldn't let anyone in her household grow the locks. She believed they were the thing of the diviners.

We sat there, Kate and I, talking about the trivialities that new lovers find so interesting. Kate kept writing notes in her journal, which was beginning to make me feel uncomfortable.

"So, have you ever met Mandela? I understand he's Kosa too?"

"Yes, he's my grandfather," I said. Traditionally speaking, I was telling the truth. Mandela shared the same clan name as my grandmother, and that made him my grandfather. But the closest I had come to meeting him was seeing him on TV.

"Oh, that's wonderful! I'd like to meet him," she said with excitement.

"No problem. I can take you there when he's in Qunu," I said. That also warranted an entry in her journal.

"So, how often do you communicate with the Mandela family? I mean, why don't they assist with your schooling?" she asked.

"You know what our people say," I said, trying to think of a way out. "Men don't talk when their mouths are full. So I don't wanna bother them," I said thoughtfully. She gave me a sympathetic kiss. I held her in my arms and for a while we were locked in a tight embrace.

Orange sunrays hid behind the mountains. The sun was done with the business of the day. We also had to make our way back before it got too dark.

When we got to Kate's room on campus, she dropped the backpack, took her towel and toiletry bag, and headed for the bathroom to take a shower. I needed to take a shower too. Walking up the mountain next to a horse in scorching heat had left my body sticky and my balls itchy. But it was a women's residence, and since the eye is a thief and the heart a follower, entering the bathroom was a risky business. I looked in the mirror to see if there was anything screaming that I had not washed. I noticed dry lips, which betrayed something else – hunger.

I opened the fridge and found two fat-free yoghurts. I opened one, looked around for a teaspoon, and couldn't see any. The business of eating should not depend on irresponsible teaspoons, I said to myself. I drank the yoghurt. It was the most tasteless yoghurt I had ever eaten, but it was quite filling. I licked the container afterwards. At that moment there was a scuffling of keys at the door. It swung open, and Kate entered with a towel wrapped above her breasts.

"Sorry it took so long. I've been sweating all day," she said.

"It's okay," I said.

"I like your white moustache, by the way." She was smiling again. I jumped to the mirror, and saw the remnants of the yoghurt around my mouth.

"Are you hungry?" she asked the obvious.

"I only had that snack today," I said.

"You didn't have breakfast? You should've told me," she said, and gave me a hug. Her touch was enough to banish all the hunger and tiredness. I untied the towel and it fell on the ground. Her breasts were small and firm. She had pink nipples that looked straight at me. They were remarkably different to what I was used to. Nonzwakazi's breasts were brown and voluptuous. She was somewhere in the villages of Mqanduli, while I was visiting the Garden of Eden with my white Eve. What if Nonzwakazi was doing the same with a new bloody Adam?

The thought ruined all the sensation that engulfed me at that moment. I tried to forge on so I would have something worthwhile to talk about in the village. I kissed Kate and pushed her to the bed. She obligingly lay on her back, legs apart. I got on top of her and tried to induce an erection. For the first time in the presence of a naked woman, my south pole didn't point north. It looked south-south instead. I felt let down.

"Don't you want me, Sipho?" she asked, in a heaving voice.

"I do. I want you desperately. But in my culture, you can't have sex without having washed and eaten first," I said, making up a story.

"Why didn't you say so?" she asked, pushing me to the side.

We got up and she led me to the women's bathroom. She peeped ahead, looking this way and that, before telling me to come in. As we walked in, the shower door swung open, and a glittering brown body came out. The woman had shaved her pubic hair. She had wide voluptuous hips, round bums and a flat stomach. Her structure was almost identical with Nonzwakazi's. She greeted and walked past, a toothbrush in one hand and a wet towel draped over her shoulder, seemingly undeterred by my presence. She stood in front of the mirror to brush her teeth. Her protruding backside gave me wild imaginations. My south pole pointed north instantly. Kate pulled me out. I left my mind in the bathroom.

I took off Kate's towel as soon as we got to the room. The sexual craving was overwhelming. I fumbled in my pockets and fished out one of those free condoms provided by the government.

"No, we can't use those," Kate said, getting up and rummaging in her handbag. She took out a pack of Lovers Plus condoms and handed it over to me. I knew what to do.

Kate, the white woman, was lying on her back, naked and ready for me. Her cheeks had turned reddish. I kissed her. I felt her hair on my tongue. I tried to remove it, and she pressed my buttocks towards her. I wanted to call all my ancestors to come and witness the work of democracy.

In a few minutes, I was lying on my back, heaving with exhaustion. Kate was resting her head on my chest, her hand tucked on my crotch, as if my south pole would suddenly escape.

"So, how come you do things in reverse now?" Kate asked.

"What do you mean?" I wondered.

"You made love before getting the food and the shower."

"Well, I had to accommodate your culture!" I said, laughing at my own stupidity. I played with her hair, which after our escapade was strewn all over the pillow.

"Please give me that," she said, pointing to her handbag. I stretched my hand, reached the bag, and handed it over.

She took out the pack of cigarettes and the journal. She lit a cigarette and dragged one long puff. Then she blew clouds of smoke at the ceiling while at the same time jotting something in her journal. That became her routine for the rest of the weekend!

At twelve o' clock on Monday I was sitting in the waiting room again, waiting to be called into the boardroom where the Dean was meeting with the Registrar and his deputy. Kate sat at her desk, stealing cautious glances at me. She had a permanent smile on her face, and I knew it was not the computer that gave her so much amusement. I also had visions of my own. I was reminiscing about the scintillating moments of the night before. She had a way of moving her hips up and keeping her waist suspended in the air – allowing me to reach deep inside her. That gave me unspeakable pleasure. She sent me into raptures when she crossed her legs over my back and pressed me tightly against her body. It was a moment of magic.

I heard the clucking of a hen. Kate's eyes popped out.

"Is this the right place to wait for the son of the Mzilas?" said a familiar voice, sending my pulse into a whirl. While I was still reeling from the shock of hearing the voice, my grandmother walked in. She had a box tucked under her arm. She had opened holes in the box, and the beak of a hen peeped through one of the holes. Kate jumped forward and received my grandmother with excitement.

"Splendid!" she said.

"Hallo, child," Grandmother greeted, but Kate was more interested in the hen. "This is so cute!" she said, scrutinising the bird. "Are you selling it?" she asked.

"Grandma, what are you doing here?" I barked at my own grandmother.

"I am here to see the Mzila man, what do you think?" she replied.

"Sipho, please ask her how much is the bird?" Kate intervened.

"Kate, this is my grandmother. She just came from the nearby village," I explained.

"You have a grandmother here! That's news to me!"

"You never asked," I said. At that point, Mr Kensington entered.

"Young man, I see you came with your grandmother today," he greeted in his own fashion.

"Yes, Sir. She is here to hear for herself," I tried to explain.

"Please come this way, Ma'am." Mr Kensington led us to the boardroom.

When we got to the boardroom, we found the Registrar, Mr Mzila and his deputy, Dr Mbewu, already waiting for us. Mr Mzila was a tall, large and hairy man. He wore a brightly coloured shirt of the type often worn by disciples of the Afrocentric persuasion. The massive beard that surrounded his face must have taken several decades to grow.

Dr Mbewu was standing, frantically sorting through documents in a thick file. She had a tiny figure, a light complexion adorned with red lipstick. She wore a mustard two-piece suit and a white low-cut blouse. She bent down, trying to scrutinise the papers. Her blouse gaped open, revealing a splendid view of her breasts. I watched the two yellow pears dangling in front of me like low-hanging fruit ready to be picked. She pulled out several pages and took a seat across from me. The pears disappeared from view. She nodded to the Registrar, signalling him to start.

"Ma'am, I assume you are this boy's grandmother," Mr Mzila said, opening the meeting. My grandmother started a long embarrassing narrative, giving our family history, in which poverty seemed to be the dominant phenomenon. In conclusion, she offered the hen to Mr Mzila.

"You of the Mzilas, you should know these things better that the light-skinned one that the child of my child has been talking to. We do not have big monies. With this hen we are coming to you, saying this is all we've got at our disposal. Our child is hungry for education. Allow him to receive this wealth of knowledge," she concluded.

Mr Mzila's eyes darted from me, to his deputy, the Dean and to the hen. Dr Mbewu was the first to respond.

"I am sorry that you had to come here personally, Grandma. It must have taken a lot of effort on your part. I am gonna interpret for Mr Kensington here, because he doesn't speak our language," she said, and then whispered to Mr Kensington, trying to summarise the long narrative. The three of them kept nodding their heads at regular intervals. I hoped that the nodding was in my favour. After some more whispering and nodding, Mr Mzila cleared his throat for our attention.

"Thank you, Ma'am, we are glad that you came to clarify the situation. Let us hear from the boy now. We need to get his point of view as a student in this institution."

"Thank you. You of the Mzilas, the child of my child is very clever in his head. The papers are there to show this. He deserves an opportunity to be educated," she said.

"Mr Mayekiso," Mr Mzila started with his interrogation. "We are trying to assist here. But you must also be co-operative. We would not like to see any student being excluded on financial grounds. But again, you have to pay for your education. We also have bills to settle. Now tell me, other than your grandmother, who else can help you?"

"Only the University can help, Sir. I have tried all I could elsewhere."

"Son, from where I am sitting, your appearance doesn't suggest that you cannot afford to pay for your studies. Look, people," he said, inviting his colleagues to the show.

"This boy has even got these stylish haircuts."

"Sir, I hear you were involved in the liberation struggle," I said.

"Yes, of course. What does that have to do with anything?"

"And you received military training in Zambia and the Soviet Union."

"That's right. I'm a fully fledged soldier here. I know hunger. I know how it feels to be in the trenches," he said, with a glimmer of pride.

"Your body does not show that you are a trained soldier, Sir, much as my appearance does not show that I have a poor background." The rebel in me had risen.

"Boy, what are you getting at?" He was clearly not pleased with my statement.

"I cut my own hair, Sir. That's why I have this haircut."

"All right," Dr Mbewu decided to intervene. "Perhaps you should give us a moment to speak to your grandmother alone," she said, addressing me directly. "Please take a seat in the waiting room. We'll call you in a moment."

When I got back to the waiting room, Kate was busy writing in her journal. She lifted her eyes once, and then went back to her writing. There was an uneasy quiet until Kate decided to drop the pretence. She closed the journal and challenged me. "Where's your grandmother now?"

"What business do you have with my grandmother's whereabouts?"

"Why are you such a liar, Sipho? Why didn't you tell me that you had family around here?"

"I didn't need to." I was not interested in arguing with her.

"So everything about our relationship was based on lies!"

"Don't you dare pretend you ever loved me!"

"What do you mean, I'm pretending?" Her face was turning red.

"I've always been an anthropological subject to you. You wanted an African with dreadlocks. I had to be Mandela's relation and all. Tell you what, I am not any of those things and I don't intend becoming anything but me, the way you see me now."

"I just can't believe this," she said and reached for her journal again.

"Are you gonna write just about everything that I say?" I grabbed the journal and looked at the page where she was writing. She had only written a subheading, "When Hunger is Gone." I went back to the first page, and there was the title, "Hunger." There were notes below the title, and my name featured prominently.

"You fucking spy! What are you all about, exactly?" I blurted out.

"Did you just call me a fucking spy?" Her eyebrows cringed, and her tiny nostrils flared. "Tell you what, *brother*, this fucking spy listened to your troubles when no one cared, this fucking spy got you an appointment with the Registrar when it seemed impossible, this fucking spy fed you when you were hungry – "

"Child of my child!" A voice spoke. I turned to look. My grandmother was standing in the doorway. There was no box under her arm.

"We have won!" she announced. I stood there, in the middle of the room, like a fly caught in a spiderweb. I could hear Kate's heavy breathing.

"They will let you study and give you food and accommodation. Hunger is gone!"

PART THREE

The Truth

The Truth

◆

TRUTH IS FOREVER ELUSIVE.

The quest to find the real truth about the truth is eternal. Truth is abstract. One man's truth is not always the same as the other's. It is dynamic, constantly changing like a chameleon changing colours.

Since you wrote your book, Themba, so many people have been asking me about the truthfulness of your story. Our story. Depending on how you look at it, the story could be anyone's. I have given them my take on the book, but I thought it was only fair that I also share this with you. I know you are probably wondering why they have to ask me about "your story" instead of you as the author. That's part of your problem, you've always been so self-centred and aloof that you've never been able to view things from somebody else's perspective.

Well, that's my version of the truth and it is up to you to swallow or spit it. You may have your other truth about what became of you and those around you, given the circumstances in which you found yourself. That's my point exactly. We are always on a quest to find truths beyond the truths presented to us. That's human nature, always inquisitive and never satisfied with what meets the eye. In your book, you talk about the people who surround you, including myself. God damn, you even talk about my mother! How is that your story and only yours, then?

Let me tell my version of the truth.

To begin with, quite early in your book, you portray me

as an irresponsible lad whose throbbing loins drove him to everything in a skirt. As an adult man, I come across as an opportunist who thrives on the difficulties that fellow human beings go through, particularly women. As a result, most people perceive me as a heartless sexual predator who views women as accessories to be used and discarded like condoms. You see, as a young man I did do some of these things, but of course you being you, you decided to tell selective parts of the truth. My assertion is that your story is only half the truth, and remember, "half truth is no truth".

The worst thing is that although you criticise my prowess in bedding multitudes of women, you do not reveal that you were always envious of all my sexual conquests in those days.

Oh, Themba, you were such a horny bugger. Remember when I caught you peeping through the keyhole of my bedroom door, trying to see my naked lover?

"What are you doing?" I asked while trying to repress laughter.

"I'm looking, eh … I'm looking for my book," you said nervously.

"Your book stays in the keyhole?" I said, pretending to sound angry for the benefit of my new lover, who was within earshot. You mumbled apologies and disappeared into your bedroom.

You always asked me to bring my lovers' panties to you, just to relish the thought that your brother had managed to remove them. Just holding those panties would give you inconceivable pleasure and fulfilment. But that's a story for another day. What I'm saying is that I was never the savage you portrayed me as in that book of yours. But knowing you, you wouldn't let the truth ruin a fascinating story.

I am writing this piece because I know from the pathetic

movies we watched that you are not the one for sequels. You always believed that they lacked soul. You said they were lousy, unimaginative extensions that throve on the success of original creations and performed at the expense of fresh ideas.

So I am not attempting to write a sequel here. Mine is an essential intervention to shed light on the grey areas in your narrative. I am going to reveal those aspects you conveniently left out of that book of yours.

By your own admission, Themba, truth hurts; and for once, we share a common view in this regard. But it baffles me that you did not think that I might be hurt by the appalling truths you wrote about the woman who brought me into this earth. I always considered you a brother, and my only one at that. But I wonder if I still have the mandate to call you as such after you told the whole world that you slept with my mother. You were my father's favourite nephew, and yet you announced in five thousand copies of your book that you slept with his widow.

But that's not my point. What I'm saying is that while perhaps I am no longer worthy of the label of a brother to you, at least you should have shown some respect for your uncle, with whose wife you slept. Maybe you felt somewhat triumphant about the encounter; maybe you thought this revelation would give audiences the necessary shock to push the sales of your book. Well, the book did fairly well in the market, but all the people with whom I discussed the story were disillusioned that you would so vividly describe a scene in which you betrayed your dead uncle by sleeping with his wife.

You see, maybe you felt like bragging about the encounter because it was a great achievement for you. Actually, what am I saying? I know you always boasted about every sexual conquest! You even went to the spaza shop wearing Thuli's earrings on your first night with her, just to show off in the township. Because the earrings were obviously feminine, people started giving you strange looks. So you told all and sundry, "They belong to Thuli, my girlfriend."

"Which Thuli?" the nosy gossipmongers asked.

"The beautiful one from down the road," you explained, clearly pleased with yourself. But I thought those were just boyhood tendencies fuelled by our wild fantasies of romantic relationships. Somehow they have stayed with you, and instead of you outgrowing them, they have grown in you.

Themba, you know that I've been in this game for a very long time. Please apply your mind properly. Try to think back and see if I ever did anything just for the hell of it. I've told lies, I've cheated, I've promised marriages and vanished without fulfilling my promises, but I never did those things in bad faith. To me, it was all about survival. You, on the other hand – you do things just for the sake of affirming the strong man you are trying to be. "A man among men," that's what you call yourself in your book, ironically titled *When a Man Cries*. You took advantage of a vulnerable schoolgirl, Nosipho. I do not mean to bring back the pain of realising too late that she was actually your biological child, but it is the principle that I am trying to interrogate here.

I know you went through hell when you discovered that she had Aids – after you had slept with her. I remember when you called the radio show and said you needed Pastor Zakes Mavi to pray for you. I was informed that the caller was from Grahamstown, and instantly I grew suspicious.

"Peace be with you, caller from Grahamstown," I greeted in the charismatic Christian fashion.

Silence.

"Brother from Grahamstown, are you there?" I said, perplexed.

Heavy breathing.

"My brother, talk to us and we will help ease the burden on your shoulders. The Good Life Evangelical Mission is here for you. Are you there?" I tried to persuade.

Tuhhhh…! That was the sound on the phone signalling that you had hung up.

"I'm sorry, it seems like the brother from Grahamstown has been disconnected. I hope that you will try again, my brother. God bless you!"

I knew right there and then that that was you, my brother, and I had to find a means of getting in touch with you after the show. And when I called you later on, I didn't ask whether you had called the show or not. Instead, I asked about the wellbeing of your family. It was then that the truth – or at least part of it – came to me.

"Thuli left me. She took the kids with her." The manner in which the words burst from your mouth clearly signalled that you had reached that stage where you would have shared your troubles with even a dog, if it cared to listen. Your voice told the story of a spiritually battered man, and I could sense this delirium hovering in the air. You definitely needed someone to talk to.

"Have you tried to convince her to come back home?"

"Yes, eventually I did. We had a misunderstanding, and we separated for months. I went to her to apologise, and she forgave me, but she hasn't come back to the house yet."

"What do you mean, she hasn't come back to the house after forgiving you?"

"Well, it's a long story. But it looks like it will take three months for her to decide whether to come back or not. My life is hell in the meantime. Complete hell!"

"Don't despair, my brother. Things will be all right."

"All right! Did you say all right? Is it all right when I have to make appointments to see my children? I can't even converse with Thuli any more. Our talk is routine only. I ask how she's doing, how the children are doing at school. And then we talk about the weather. Now tell me, Pastor Zakes, is it *all right* for a couple who have been married for ten years to have nothing but the weather to talk about?"

You shouted at me as if your intention was to burst my eardrum. I could hear your breath whistling in the receiver, and I realised that the situation was extremely volatile. I wouldn't have been surprised if you were already contemplating suicide.

That's when I made up my mind that I must come to Grahamstown, to be with you before you did something stupid. I was helping thousands of people who had given up on life. I thought it would be highly hypocritical of me if I didn't do the same for my brother, so I decided to pack my bags and head for the City of Saints, as they call it.

By that time my church had a membership of over ten thousand people, many of whom saw me as a Messiah. I could take advantage of those people in whatever way I wanted. Imagine, some even offered me their salaries as a way of expressing their gratitude. But I chose not to accept those offerings, refusing to take advantage of the vulnerable. It is not that I didn't need the money – hell no, I did. Everybody needs money, even the Pope! I didn't take advantage of them because beneath these priest's robes, beneath my own financial needs and sexual desires, lies a caring human being. And being humane is integral to every human being.

This was what I was trying to drum into your head when we spent those three weeks together in Grahamstown. At least you were prepared to share your story, with very stringent editing, however. "I slept with a schoolgirl and Thuli found out about it," you explained.

"A school child!" I was visibly stunned, which was not a good sign for an experienced counsellor like me. Anger welled up in my chest, but I tried to contain it, like a drunkard trying to stop himself from vomiting.

"Brother, what was wrong with you? How can you, I mean, how would you feel if another teacher did that to your own child?" I found myself shouting at you like the little brother that you are.

"Zakes, please stop it already. I've had enough of those morality lessons. The last thing I want is to go back there."

There were signs of petulance and fatigue on your face. You wanted to flush everything that happened into the labyrinth of history. But I wouldn't let you get away with it that easily.

"Okay, I'm sorry for being insensitive. You are right, let's deal with the current situation. You say the first results were negative?" I beckoned you to continue. I had to modify my approach in the interests of getting more information from you.

"Yes, they were. I'm expecting the second results next week. It is torture, I'm telling you. I always said I'd only get tested when I know for sure that there is a cure for Aids. But now it's an ultimatum that Thuli gave me: three tests over three months before she'll come back with the kids. Can you imagine that, spending whole three months with the scary thought that the results might assert that I'm HIV-positive?"

"At least Thuli is prepared to continue with the marriage. I do quite a lot of counselling for couples, and I've seen worse cases."

"Please don't come with that pastor nonsense now. You don't know what I've been through."

"Why don't you tell me what you've been through, then? Brother to brother."

"Well, where do I start?"

"From the beginning."

"*Ag* man, you know what I mean." We burst out laughing simultaneously. That was a good icebreaker, I said to myself.

And then you went on and told me the story of your association with the young girl; how her health had deteriorated, how she found out about her HIV status. You told me that she had confided in Thuli as a social worker. That was when Thuli decided to leave you. You also told me how you dropped your pride and begged Thuli to forgive you. And Thuli forgave you, with the condition that you should get tested for HIV. As you narrated your tale, I felt as if I was listening to a retired prostitute telling her life story on the last day of her impending departure from this world. Or a witch confessing all her witchcraft activities as she gasped her last breath.

But the strangest thing is that only Thuli had a clear identity in your story. You never mentioned the girl's name, where she lived, her family, or anything else about her life. What I knew about her was only your encounter and her medical condition. I wanted you to stop thinking about the Aids test results all the time, because whether you had contracted the virus or not, nothing would have made what you did to this Nosipho right. I'm saying it again: raping is never a good thing, no matter how anyone tries to justify it.

I'm sorry I'm going back to this, but I just wanted you to think seriously about the way you treat other human beings. I wanted to revitalise in your conscience a sense of respect for human dignity and the value of life. When I advised you to write down everything, I didn't mean you should go ahead and publish it! Writing can be therapeutic, and I wanted you to use it as a catharsis, for the sake of your own mental stability, not as a financial venture. I know you called it a novel, but everybody can now see the real story through that thin veil of fiction. You did not even have the decency to show me the draft before taking it to the publishers. And I had to read from newspaper reviews about your sexual encounter with my mother.

Perhaps you thought that was the most shocking encounter a young man could have. Unfortunately that is not the case. We all have moments that astonish, but some of them are just too despicable to write about. The act of copulation with your aunt is not in itself out of the ordinary; boys often have their first sexual encounters with older women, anyway. And those women are usually people close to them. They can either be helpers in their homes, neighbours' children, or even visiting relatives. The only thing that raises eyebrows about your story is that you used it as a gimmick to get noticed within the literary fraternity. "Here comes the writer who slept with his own aunt," some will say when they attend your public readings.

I have my own shocking stories as well, but I don't intend to exploit them for the sake of fame and fortune. But I must nevertheless tell you that I made a lot of sacrifices for you to be where you are today, both as a family man and the successful writer that you have become.

You know that Thuli was not exactly a virgin when you met her. Yeah, that's right! I deflowered Thuli. She was my girlfriend, but I was impressed that my otherwise cowardly brother was, for the first time in his life, courageous enough to declare undying love for a girl, and I decided to sacrifice her for you. It was not that easy, though. I had to convince Thuli that you would be a better lover while I tried by all means to discredit myself as an ideal boyfriend. Do you remember that I suddenly had a string of girlfriends in a short period of time? It wasn't because I enjoyed the Casanova lifestyle; I was trying to prove to Thuli that I was not to be trusted. In that way, I pushed her straight into your arms.

You made me proud when you finally snatched her, but you took forever. Remember that first day I left you both in the classroom? I told her that I had wanted us to meet in that classroom, but I planned to leave the two of you there. You know, sometimes girls end up with people not only because they love them, but because they spend a lot of time around them; they get used to them, and end up accepting them. Thuli had to accept you because I went further and further away, while you were always there for her. Having accepted you, she had to teach herself to also love you. That wasn't too difficult, because there is a sprinkling of natural charm in you. But your overt shyness was a drawback. She was disappointed that you would not even maintain eye contact with her, even though you walked together from school most of the time.

"He's a shy chap; you must be patient with him," I had urged her, but she was really losing patience with you. When that happens, girls usually submit to the overtures of the next boy who crosses their path, and I didn't want this to happen to you.

I had to do something to ensure that she didn't fall into the wrong hands, so I kept her warm from time to time until the day you both shared the fruit from the Garden of Eden. I could see from the smile across your face that from that day on, you were no longer "pure". On that day we could hardly finish our homework because you wanted to tell me about the strange feeling in your crotch, and the rapid jerking movements that were coupled with an uncontrollable and powerful ejaculation. You said you wanted to eject and release outside of her because you were embarrassed that she'd say you peed into her thing. But it seemed like she was possessed with some demons of her own as she pressed you down against her body. I explained what was going on to you, and you promised to prove yourself the following day.

Thuli was always a faithful girl, but even the most faithful can be prone to the first love syndrome. Every time they come across impediments in their youthful romantic fantasies, they find themselves crawling back to the one crowned for having invaded their girlhood nests for the first time. So it happened that Thuli confided in me that you lasted for approximately the duration of a fowl's intercourse. Whereas I would take her to cloud nine and beyond, you only took her to cloud three before collapsing. So I had to do what any caring and capable man would do.

I'm glad that eventually you were prepared to let her lead the way, and so she taught you all the things we used to do together. But maybe it was a little too late. Thuli was already pregnant. Yes, she was pregnant with Nozizwe. I'm sorry you had to learn about it this way, but hey, what's the best way to break that kind of news? After all, I found out about your tryst with my mother in a national newspaper – that wasn't the best way, was it?

Please don't be angry at Thuli. She always wanted to tell you this, but I advised her against it because I was trying to save your fragile heart. Do you remember her remark after finding out that Nosipho was actually your biological child? Of course you do, because you wrote about it in *When a Man Cries*. You wrote that she said she had always wondered why Thembi looked so much like Nosipho. Well, you should understand that Nosipho and I come from the same womb and that makes her my half-sister, and therefore there was a resemblance between her and my child. Thank you for being a good father to my daughter.

As I said, I thought I was being sensitive to your feelings, but your one-sided account in your book gave me no choice but to pen my version of the truth. I hope that one day Thuli will find the courage to pour out her heart and let the whole world know that two sides of the story are not always enough. There are just too many truths to be told.

The Other Truth

◆

WHAT IS WRONG WITH MEN these days? You know, even the most manly man can behave in a manner that leaves you cold with shock and disappointment. Zakes is a streetwise dude, and surely not the kind you would expect to spread rumours like a lousy village herald. And now the same Zakes tells all and sundry blatant lies, with the sole purpose of trying to repair his dented public image.

Let me set the record straight: what Zakes says in his story is not entirely true. Yes, as a young and naïve girl I experimented with him when we were teenagers. Who doesn't know that as part of growing up, teenagers tend to be rebellious and take risks, for crying out loud? Of course, at that stage you are still impressionable. You live in a world of fantasy that can sometimes propel you into embracing any fool that comes your way. Since there is no formula for choosing partners, many young girls find themselves saying "yes" to some pervert just because they feel pity for him. The next thing he runs after every skirt in sight, beating his chest and claiming that he is "the man". I know this because I learned the hard way.

It happened to me when I started courting sexual explorations with Zakes. It was very naïve of him to have considered that as falling in love. Those escapades came from nothing more than childish infatuation and conforming to peer pressure. I am disappointed that at his age, Zakes has not yet realised the intricacies of growing up.

Perhaps it's because Zakes has never grown up. He is the only forty-year-old teenager I know. What kind of a man brags about having absconded from his paternal responsibilities for over thirteen years? As soon as I told him about the damage his seed had done in me, his impulse was to deny everything, as if he was not capable of creating a baby. When the pregnancy corresponded with the date of our last sexual encounter and he could not deny any more, he pleaded with me not to tell anyone. Before I knew, he had vanished in the thin air. Of course, he claimed that he was going to Joburg to find a job and send me *papgeld* for the baby.

I did not believe him, but I had to let him go. Although Themba had good promise in life, he was only completing high school at the time, and I did not want to frustrate him by revealing that the child was not his. I found myself with no other option but to let Themba unknowingly front for his irresponsible brother. At the time, I was oblivious to the depth of the trap that I would fall into. I should have known that the best that Zakes could offer were empty promises.

"Thuli, I will find a good job and give you all the support you need. I promise," Zakes had said, trying to get me out of his face.

"But what am I gonna do with a fatherless child?" I had wondered.

"There's no such thing as a fatherless child. As long as there are men out there, you can't speak of the scarcity of fathers. You can find a father for the baby."

"What do you mean? You are the father, why do I have to run around looking for a substitute father when I know exactly who the father of my child is?"

"Look, Thuli, you know very well that Themba won't take to this easily. Now, allow him the right to be the father until I find a good job. After all, we are the same blood. This arrangement will be accepted even in the ancestral world." There was truth in what he was saying, but I also knew that Zakes did not care about Themba's feelings. He only cited them for his own convenience. I had to compromise because I cared about Themba, and didn't want to see him suffer. Besides, giving birth to a fatherless child was and still is regarded a highly abominable act and a disgrace to society.

And off Zakes went to the City of Gold, where he hoped to find a decent job that would earn him enough money to take care of his paternal responsibilities – or so he said. As soon as he set his foot in Johannesburg, his purpose changed dramatically. Now his priority was to find the next heart he could break. And what followed was another bunch of children littering this land of our forefathers. Now the poor children are strewn all over like little seeds during the sowing season; but unlike crops, many of these unfortunate children are withering before they can even grow. They are dying of hunger because their mothers are left to fend for themselves without help from the man who was party to their creation.

What is fatherhood if all a man does is plant the seed and vanish with his name? Is such a man worth calling a father? To me, he is nothing more than a sperm donor. Such a man has no business claiming fatherhood to my child. He does not have a rightful claim to manhood, either. The little organ between his legs only affirms his maleness; manhood is far more than that. It is earned, and it comes with responsibility.

I am glad that my little Nozi is doing well without Zakes in her life. Perhaps it's about time Zakes understood that fatherhood is not just the ability to break an ovum. But again, it takes a reasonable man to realise that, and unfortunately Zakes is not remotely close to being reasonable. In fact, I can hardly find anything he is good for, other than breaking the hearts of vulnerable women.

I wish men could understand the pain they cause single mothers.

I am looking forward to the day the Creator turns things around and puts men in our shoes. Won't that be great, having several men to yourself, and they all know that you are cheating, and your weapon of defence is denial? As long as you are not caught red-handed, you deny association with all the men in your life even though there's plenty of evidence to prove it.

In the meantime, these men clean the house, bathe the children and bring you food while you are busy watching soccer and drinking beer with friends. Afterwards you get to bed late with cold feet, start caressing them and demanding your conjugal rights. You force them to kiss your ashtray-smelling mouth while they are trying to catch up with sleep after a long day of taking care of you and your children.

And there comes the time when you must be nursed just because you are suffering from a cold after a night out with "the boys". Isn't it pathetic, the way a cold is a serious ailment to men? They begin to tremble and call their mothers from the villages, just because you are not sensitive to their feelings. Now, who doesn't know that a cold lasts for about five days, after which one will be back on one's feet? (Literally for men, because the only time they stay in their houses and get to know the inside of their bedrooms is when they are sick.) But five days is too long for men, and they begin to act as if they can already see the gates of Heaven opening and Gabriel ushering them to the next world.

Could they ever stand the menstrual pains that we are

subjected to every month? What about labour pains? They can't even watch you giving birth to their own children. Several of the few brave men who do gather courage to be in the labour wards pass out at the sight of blood heralding the arrival of their own babies.

But having said that, not all men are as irresponsible as the supposed "father of my child". I feel bad that I had to lie to Themba, because he certainly did not deserve this deception. Lies generate more lies until they are well out of control. It was through lies that I compromised my relationship, and what could have been a great matrimony between Themba and me.

People can say whatever they like about Themba, but my husband is a great man. He's got weaknesses, of course, just like the rest of us. And his brother, please, no one can tell me a thing about Zakes. He is propaganda incarnated, a true manifestation of lies and the epitome of charlatanism. Even that is not enough to describe the man who portrays himself as the "conveyor of truth".

I have seen Zakes with my own eyes deceiving women into believing that he owns a construction company, whereas the truth is that he used to lift a pick and the shovel on the mines. Isn't he the same man who led poor Miss Phatheka into resigning her job as the principal of Sinethemba High School, with the prospect of moving to Johannesburg where he was supposed to have found her a better job? And guess what Zakes did as soon as she gave up her job? He disappeared two days before their wedding day, and the poor woman's heart almost stopped!

And now that same man has the audacity to call my husband names just because he is the so-called pastor of a charismatic church, and he thinks he's got the front row in the next world. Oh please, pastor my left foot; a dog will always be a dog!

The signs are already showing, and soon everybody will see Zakes's true colours. His loins are as troublesome as ever. In fact, it is fascinating that he became a born-again Christian in prison. Can you believe it, a man who was arrested for defrauding the state of social grants now thinks himself fit to criticise everyone else? The money he stole was meant for orphans, many whose parents had died of Aids-related diseases. Now tell me, what kind of a man steals from the poor and puts the lives of children at risk, just like that?

He had managed to manoeuvre his way out of prison, of course. But it is interesting to note that his release had nothing to do with his innocence, and more to do with needing to catch a bigger fish than him. This is the classical irony of our justice system, acquitting criminals in exchange for information that would incriminate a more appetising criminal. The so-called "big fish" was his live-in partner, Lerato Mohapi, who is the mother of his three children – the lovely twins and their equally beautiful younger sister. What could be more cowardly than a man who gets the mother of his children locked up behind bars just to save his own skin?

Lerato was a senior official in the Department of Social Security in charge of orphan funds, which began to disappear like morning dew on a hot summer's day. It is unclear whether Zakes started courting her affections precisely because he knew she was a potential reservoir of public funds, but it soon became evident that the taxpayers' money had vanished, unaccounted for. He lived a lavish lifestyle, and it became as clear as the back of a white goat moving up the hill that his fountain of funds never ran dry through all the seasons. The long arm of the law, led by the Chairperson of the Scrape Committee, Mr Gideon Themba, finally caught up with Zakes. It was quite strategic for Parliament to appoint a politician with nothing to lose to this committee, as Mr Themba is the only Member of Parliament in his party. His sting has no bounds; no wonder he barely has any following.

The Scrape stung Zakes after he was caught with a stack of birth certificates with which he had registered children for orphan grants despite the fact that most of their parents were alive and well-off. Apparently, he was pocketing the money every month. It was clear that somebody in the government structure had been assisting Zakes in that fraudulent operation. So although Zakes was jailed for five years, after only seven months he turned state witness.

Now seven months is even less than the normal term of pregnancy, and yet this man could not endure a few months behind bars. Of course, his claim was that he was now "a changed man, a new man, a born-again Christian", and that not telling the truth was against the will of God.

Before anyone could realise it, Zakes was standing in front of the magistrate pleading innocence and promising to reveal the truth about the social grants scam.

"Your Worship, I will tell the whole truth, nothing but the truth."

"You promise the whole truth this time?"

"Yes, your Worship. The whole truth." To him, truth meant putting the blame squarely on the mother of his children. And so he gave his version of the truth, thus digging a grave for the poor woman.

Everyone knew that if Zakes had been a victim, he was a willing one. Why else would he go around collecting birth certificates that were then used for deceitful purposes? No one was holding a bayonet to his head those days he went to withdraw money from his bank account – which boasted huge figures, even though he did not have a job. He was the envy of many when he wore designer suits, drove flashy cars, and played golf with the rich and famous of Johannesburg. He knew that he was leading a criminal life, and he should therefore have been prepared to face the consequences. But not Zakes Mavi. He may not be politically connected, but he sure knows how to get himself out of trouble.

Zakes, a man with a taste for the good things in life – beautiful women, a luxurious lifestyle and no academic qualification other than a criminal record – was now out of prison. What could such a man do to earn a living? The church was the obvious alternative. Those who know say the Bible is the only book that criminals like him have free access to in the prison cells. Apparently Zakes read the holy text with such great relish that he was able to convert some hard-nosed criminals into becoming born-again Christians. It is said that that was how he managed to escape being somebody's "wife" in prison.

Zakes is now a free man preaching the word of God while the mother of his children is serving a fifteen-year jail sentence.

Now what kind of a man gets his woman to commit crime, enriches himself through her wrong-doing, and leaves her to rot in jail while he preaches righteousness to the world?

Oh, Lord behold, I will never trust Zakes. And he can forget about being a father to my child. My little Nozi is now in Grade 8 – she has gone this far without Zakes, she doesn't need him. Like a desperate female dog, I had to wander around holding my little girl with my teeth in an effort to prepare a better world for her.

Zakes was gallivanting in the City of Gold while I was dispatched to the villages of Transkei because I had fallen pregnant as a teenager. A township girl from a family of relative substance had to be concealed in an obscure village with no electricity and only a pit hole for a toilet. I had to learn to use candlelight for reading and to master the art of smearing cow dung on the floor of the hut where I slept with several cousins I had never known before. I learned anew the meaning of the word poverty, while my grandmother taught me the concept of sharing.

"Child of my child," my grandmother had said. "You must understand that siblings share a locust's head at times of difficulty."

"A locust's head, Grandma?"

"Yes, child of my child, you must learn to settle for whatever is available. I'm just a pensioner and sometimes we don't even have a drop of water here. Here is not like in the cities where you get water from taps," she said.

I had to follow the tails of cattle, eager to have them dropping their waste. I had to learn to milk smelly goats in order to feed my baby. I fed my baby goat-milk as an alternative to breastfeeding. If I must be grateful to a man, it is to the he-goat that got my grandmother's she-goat pregnant, because that way I was able to feed Nozi.

But you know what, I don't regret all the hardship I went through trying to raise my daughter. Everything happens for a reason, they say. I believe there was good reason why all of this happened to me. I learned to be grateful, to appreciate life, and be content with what I had. As my soul sister, Lira, the songstress from Daveyton, puts it, "maybe we fall so we can watch ourselves begin to rise again."

Falling pregnant from a meaningless encounter was the deepest fall indeed, but I gained a lot from that experience. At times, we acquire wisdom from the most unfortunate circumstances. To acquire anything of value, one must sacrifice something. My heart was broken, and I lost my blood to have a wonderful daughter in Nozi. It was worth it. It also strengthened my resolve to study and finish my Social Work degree in record time.

Today I am an independent woman with my own choices to make. Those choices include deciding what kind of man I want to spend the rest of my life with. Some still wonder why a smart and successful woman like me would accept a man back after it became abundantly clear that he had committed adultery with an HIV-positive girl. Well, wonder no more, because I know what I want. I love Themba, and I want him in my life. I always have. It's as simple as that.

Remember, when I left him, I made it clear that I would accept him back only when he agreed to test for HIV. Tell me, was Themba the first man to cheat? If you marry someone with the purpose of growing old with him, would you sacrifice your marriage just because he cheated? Already we have a surplus of divorces. Imagine if everyone turned to divorce after their husbands were implicated in some meaningless sexual encounter!

I gave Themba an ultimatum when I left, and now he has acceded to my demands. My plan was not to unleash my fury randomly and indefinitely. The only thing I would have gained would have been to see him suffer momentarily; and then I would have lived a life full of regrets. I did not want the sweetest moments of my life – especially moments with my children – to haunt me as a constant and bitter reminder of what used to be. The happiest moments hurt more than the miserable experiences when they are located in a distant past that cannot be revisited.

Sometimes it is good when a man admits his guilt, and you don't have the kind of reaction he expected. That's the best way to deal with them, because then they are wary, wondering how the punishment will be executed. They become cautious with every step they take. They won't sneeze without your permission, and even report to you when they want to go to the toilet.

Besides, in any kind of reconciliation (unless it is brokered by a South African bishop with a squeaky voice), the former victim must emerge more powerful than the perpetrator. Accepting Themba back meant that I was now in control of our relationship. Right now, I tell him when to take the HIV test; I determine his visiting hours to see the children; and when he may call me and when not. Now I am in charge. I have already collected my third HIV test result, but I told the doctor to hold Themba's back for a while. I want to keep him anxious while he continues to worship the ground on which I set my foot. There is something liberating about having power over a man.

Yes, I am an independent woman, but I also have needs. I have known Themba since high school; that must be well over twenty years now. I love him. And as more than just a lover; I cherish his companionship and gentlemanly demeanour. No one understands me and comforts me the way Themba does. And I'm afraid no one ever will. I don't want an almost-Themba kind of guy when I can have the real Themba.

All was well with Themba until he had too much money. Indeed, money is the devil's plan to spoil the purest of hearts. Money broke my marriage. It was after acquiring monetary wealth that Themba started running after young girls. But money does not have brains. Human beings do. I would never allow money to destroy the humanity in me. Matrimonial life is just too precious to be ruined by money.

Themba may have gone astray, but he is finding his way back into my arms. We all falter at times, but a good man knows where the Creator placed his missing rib. Themba watched his brother boasting about his sexual conquests.

It is clear today that he was envious of his brother, but was incapable of being a "playa" at the time.

Maybe it is best that we leave playing to the "playas", as young people refer to womanisers these days. Yes, some men think we are mere objects for playing with. Toys. The boyhood tendency of gathering as many toys as possible manifests itself as men grow older. They collect women as toys to play with, and then they discard them. They are heartless – anyone doing that does not deserve to be called human.

Infidelity has its requirements. Not just anyone can venture into licentious ways. It needs a special skill – the art of lying. If you are endowed with the art of weaving together snippets of truths with the blankest of faces, you are likely to have a longer lifespan as a "playa". Zakes is such a man. A good liar knows that a little bit of truth can transform the most blatant of lies into something compellingly believable. It is no wonder that Zakes now uses my little Nozi to mask his misdeeds over the years. Now he even hides behind the Bible, as if that will suddenly erase everything from the public memory.

Today his three children have joined the hundreds of thousands of orphans in this country, even though he is still alive. Since their mother was arrested, the children had to be taken to an orphanage – while he was busy criss-crossing the country preaching the word of God!

Zakes is an accomplished liar. He is so obsessive about fabricating stories that he starts believing them. My deeply religious parents would probably rebuke me for this, but the decisions of the God of today leave a lot to be desired. I wish for the return of the God of the Old Testament, whose vengeance would teach the likes of Zakes a lesson they will never forget for the rest of their miserable lives.

I wish God had invented Aids for a good reason – to

punish those who deserve it most. The disease now kills innocent children, and leaves others parentless. There are more deserving candidates – like Zakes, who would be first in line if Aids was designed for people who have earned it the most. These are my true sentiments.

So Many Truths

◆

THERE IS A MOUSE IN my house.

It stays in the kitchen. It goes to the living room sometimes. It visits my bedroom, too. It has been to every corner of my house. It knows my house better than I do.

It leaves a trail of droppings everywhere it goes. There are heaps of droppings in every room of my house. Some droppings are moist and shiny, others look grey and dull and they feel hard in my hands. I started counting the droppings the other day. I was on the 179th when my phone rang. I answered the phone, but it turned out to be a wrong number. I could not remember which dropping I had last counted before the phone call. But I knew for sure that if I could convert rat shit into money, I would become a multimillionaire.

The mouse is in my house. I hear its sound when it grinds my food. The sound changes as it moves from one object to another. It eats and shits at the same time. Such a callous creature! I even find its droppings in the bread bin. I do not clean rat shit. Who can expect me to clean up after an irksome rodent that has been pissing on my food, spreading its shit all over and eating everything that it comes across, including clothes?

I had an encounter with the mouse this morning. It was trapped in a box of cornflakes that I had thrown into the rubbish bin after dinner last night. I had had the cornflakes for lunch yesterday. I had them for breakfast before that. It is not that I am incapable of cooking my own food. I just don't have time to waste in the kitchen. What if I catch fire while busy dangling my beard over the simmering pots?

I went to bed after having cornflakes for supper last night. I was awoken by the sound that I initially thought was a knock at the door. I later realised that it was indeed a knock. Only that it was not a knock from a visitor, and not at the door. It was a knock from a fellow resident and practically the co-owner of my house. It was a knock from the mouse trying to find its way out of the box of cereal.

I saw the mouse in the box.

I took a broom ready to smash it into smithereens. I could already visualise blood splashing all over the box, the floor and the walls. I would squash even its head. Only mouse mince-meat would be left as remnants of a mouse life that was. I took a look at it before laying down the gauntlet. The little piece of mammal that had been destroying my nights for over a month was sitting nervously at the bottom of the box. It seemed so helpless. Its eyes stood out like black beads at the corners of its face. Its back had brown, shiny lines. And its tail was thick and long. It looked healthy and strong. It was well nourished from my food.

I thought of all the sacrifices that were made for me and all the difficulties that I went through to live a decent life. My uneducated parents sacrificed the little money they got from their farm workers' wages to send me to school so that I could become somebody one day. I studied hard to finish school and get a degree. I wake up every morning to go to work so that I can have a place to stay, eat well and live a good life. And this rodent gets all of that for free – and shits on my food afterwards.

As I was holding the broomstick ready to thrash the living daylights out of the bloody rodent, my mind shuttled between the past, the present and the future. Old man

Jongilanga's words resonated in my head. He once told me that any man who fights someone who does not fight back is a coward. I tried to imagine life after the death of the rodent. I thought about the agonising silence that was there before there was a mouse in my house. I would listen to my own breathing, the rumbling of my own stomach and the grinding of my own teeth. There was no sound unless I made it. Now I was about to kill the only other creature that gave life to my house.

I turned the box upside down, and the mouse landed on the floor. I remained transfixed as it ran nervously towards the wall before making a U-turn and going between my legs. I instinctively jumped in fright, then laughed at the absurdity of my actions. Just a moment ago the creature's life was in my hands, and already I was scared of it. I turned to look and saw its tail turning the corner. That was the last I saw of the mouse.

My house has become a lonely cave since my separation from my family. My wife took the children with her when she decided that I was not fit to live with her. But yesterday I had the opportunity to spend time with my family. I wanted to hold up the sun.

Since our separation, my wife has never been to our home, not until yesterday. It was Thembi's birthday, our last-born daughter. Yes, I surprised myself by remembering. I am notorious for forgetting people's birthdays. I have been in trouble for it, particularly with my wife. She does not take kindly to such things. Thembi was turning five, and next year she will be going to school. As a responsible father I decided to do something to celebrate my daughter's birthday. But Thuli had bigger plans.

I called Thuli for the usual appointment. Yes, I still see my wife and children only by appointment. It is almost a year since I was accused of having molested an HIV-positive school girl – Nosipho. She died, poor Nosipho. She died of an Aids-related sickness. I never knew that she was a carrier of the virus when I slept with her. I never knew that she was my daughter either. It was only when she was dying that I became aware of all of this. This was good enough reason for my wife to leave our matrimonial home. She took our two girls with her. All of this is weighing down on me.

I have since taken three HIV tests. To my relief, the results came out negative, at least for the first two of them. The third result is taking a little longer than I expected. I am still waiting for the phone call to tell me it is ready. This result is crucial to me, because it is only once I get it that my stubborn wife will decide whether or not she is returning to our home with the kids. In the meantime, I'm suffering.

She agreed that we could meet the following day, which was a Sunday. But she said I should not come to her aunt's place, where she is living with our children. She did not want to come to our house either. She said we should meet at the park. A separated husband and wife meeting at the park! We are adults, so I could not understand why we had to meet in some park as if we were having a secret affair. But I could not say this to her in case she changed her mind and refused to meet with me.

When I got to the park, she was not there. Just as I was beginning to get edgy, a new BMW X3 drove in and parked next to my red Citi Golf.

"There's daddy!" That was Nozi's voice. I was overwhelmed as I saw the love and excitement in my daughter's eyes. Yes, Nozizwe is my daughter, no matter what people say. I am aware that Zakes, my sorry excuse for a brother, wrote some lousy piece claiming that Nozizwe was his. Where was he when she was born? Does he even know the meaning of fatherhood? I am not going to dignify Zakes's erroneous claims with a response. He certainly does not deserve my time and energy.

Zakes developed an allergy to the truth from an early age. What he does not understand is that lies perpetuate more lies. When lying has infiltrated a man's system, he begins to find it difficult to distinguish between fact and fiction. His notions of truth become blurred. His conceptual understanding of truth becomes an abstract phenomenon. That is why my so-called brother is such a stranger to the truth.

Here in front of me was my daughter – and that would never change. I immediately got out of the car. Nozi was already running to me, with Thembi in hot pursuit. I stretched my arms, picked her up and held Nozi to my height before kissing her. It was only after the kiss that I remembered that Thuli might not approve of my actions. Since I had been accused of molesting my own child – my illegitimate child, a child I never knew I had fathered – everyone was extra cautious around me. I would not have taken offence if Thuli felt uncomfortable with me giving lip kisses to the children.

Thembi was standing in front of me with her arms held up high. "Me too, me too, Daddy," I heard her plead. I shifted Nozi to my right arm and lifted Thembi with my left. "Ah, you are so heavy. What does Mummy feed you?"

"All the nice foods," she said with glee.

"Oh, that one doesn't want to eat," remarked Thuli, between light giggles.

"Me, I eat all my food, Daddy," boasted Thembi.

"Do you? Well done, my girl. You'll be strong if you eat all your food."

"Me too, I'm strong!"

"Okay, okay, you are gonna break Daddy's back now.

Why don't you two ride your bicycles over there?" I did not even notice that Thuli was struggling, trying to push the two bicycles. I put the two girls down with the hope of assisting my wife, but it was too late. The two girls grabbed their bicycles and climbed onto them instantly. It was really unbelievable to see even the youngest one riding a bicycle with ease. I only managed to ride a bicycle once I was already in my teens, and I bruised my thighs several times before being able to ride it properly.

"Why are you smiling so much?" Thuli's question knocked me back to the present.

"It's so good to see these little ones so happy," I said. Thuli released her usual light giggle.

"Are you gonna assist me here or not?" It was only then that I noticed the bag of charcoal and a *braai* stand next to the car.

"I'm sorry. I didn't notice that you brought those," I said as I grabbed the *braai* stand and walked alongside Thuli as our eyes searched for the best picnic spot.

"What did you think we were gonna do at the park, have sex?" She noticed the embarrassment on my face. I had not talked to Thuli about that kind of stuff since our separation.

We found a spot and I prepared the fire. Whoever invented *braai* briquettes is a genius. I was always useless on the home front. Even though I was born on a farm where there was no electricity, I never really had to make fire because my parents were there, and I was too young at the time. Thuli's stay in the villages during her first pregnancy made her a better fire-maker than me. I spread the briquettes and blitz on the *braai* stand and gingerly lit a match. The briquettes caught fire immediately. I sat in the bench side-by-side with my wife and watched the red flames growing.

"How are they doing at school?" I started a new conversation.

"They are doing all right," she said summarily.

"Yeah?" I tried to urge her on.

"Nozi is doing well with all her other subjects, but is struggling a bit with Maths."

"And Thembi?" I probed further.

"She's doing all right. She's doing ballet and she's really enjoying it," she spoke with a mixture of confidence and pride.

"Ballet! Black kids do ballet these days?"

"Why not? She does it better than many white kids."

"You mean my girl wears those shoes that look like a pig's nose?"

"Ballet shoes. She spins like magic in them!"

There was a momentary silence.

"And you? I mean, you really look good. Are you seeing, I mean, how's life?"

"You want to know if I'm seeing anyone." She was smiling.

"Yeah, something like that," I said hesitantly.

"So, you think I shouldn't be looking good if I'm not seeing anyone?"

"Actually, what I really want to know is, eh, how is life. You know what I mean."

"Life is good. I got a promotion last month."

"Really! That's…" I got tongue-tied for a moment. "That's, eh, congratulations," I said half-heartedly. Thuli probably noticed this. In all honesty, I was not sure whether to be happy or not for her because progress on her part could disadvantage me. Who would want to be with a stagnant man? Her promotion was a nasty reminder that I tended to be an underachiever. This is the trouble when a man marries high. You are constantly challenged and put under pressure to prove yourself financially, intellectually and, sometimes, physically.

"Thank you," she said after a momentary pause.

I had to cut to the chase before I ran out of things to say. I asked her what I could get for Thembi's birthday.

"Actually, I've got a better idea."

"And that is?" I asked.

"Why don't we organise a party at home?"

"At home?"

"Yes, at our house. Do you have a problem with that?"

"That would be great!" I could not believe what my ears were hearing.

"Are you sure?" she asked.

"Most definitely. It will be wonderful to have all of you back home." I could not conceal my excitement.

"Only for the day of the party, though. I can hire jumping castles and we can invite her schoolmates and friends from the neighbourhood."

"For sure. That's a brilliant idea."

We spent the rest of the afternoon going down memory lane. We reminisced about the good old days. She wondered why, when I was still courting her, I had resorted to writing letters in my deficient English. She still kept some of those letters, and I was not always proud to hear letters of yesteryear being read back to me. We laughed. We touched. And there was a rush of blood to my southern hemisphere. The desire to have her in my arms was irrepressible. The wish to share the best of my loving was phenomenal. To watch my children playing was blissful.

Driving back from the park that afternoon, I didn't feel like going back to the empty house. I stopped at old man Jongilanga's. Everything seemed to have a peculiar character in old man Jongilanga's home. Things like his walking-stick, his chair, and even his dog – all had something unique about them. The dog came out first, wagging its tail. It started sniffing my legs and when I tried to push it with my hand, it licked it. It was a happy soul. So was I.

"Knock, knock! Is there anyone at home?"

"We are here, we are here, son of AmaMpandla," responded the old man.

"I greet you, old man," I said as I walked in.

"Greetings, greetings, my son." The old man got up to shake hands. His chair faced the street. He probably saw me coming from a distance. "Please squat here, my son," he said, ushering me to a seat.

"Thank you, old man," I said, pulling the chair to sit.

"How is health, my son?" Now he was resting both his hands on his walking-stick, which stood in front of him. The handle of the walking-stick was decorated with a sculpture of a human face, which he unconsciously suffocated with his hands. Old man had carved it himself.

"We have woken, old man."

"Go on, son," he said nodding slowly.

"The weather is beautiful."

"I hear you, my son."

"How is it going with you, old man?" He was expecting me to prolong my health report, but unfortunately I was never articulate in that respect. I knew that in his report, old man could move from telling you about his health and presenting the weather report to giving you a lecture about his family tree, including the birth of dogs and donkeys.

"The coughs never stop, my son."

"Yes, old man."

"We live with our sicknesses."

"Yes, old man."

"We walk in our ill-health."

"Walk in ill-health, old man."

"We carry all the problems on our shoulders and move along with them day after day, night after night. They have become an indispensable burden in our lives."

"Yes, old man."

"We drag like branches those that we cannot carry along."

"Yes, old man."

"We have been struck by eternal drought."

"Eternal drought, old man."

"Meanwhile, there has been abundance of rain in the land of the fish. They even plant in stones there."

"Planting in stone, old man." I kept echoing his words.

"My son says torrents of rain sweep away houses there, just like in the time of Noah." At that moment, old man Jongilanga's wife emerged from the kitchen with a tray of tea.

"Greetings, Mama."

"Hey, son of my neighbour, your baboon gallops very well."

"You think so, Mama?"

"Yes, you got here just as I was preparing tea." She served us the tea, and I had to follow the ritual of drinking even though I am not much of a tea person.

"You look good, my son," old man Jongilanga said while dipping a teaspoon in a sugar basin.

"Thank you, old man," I said with not much interest in explaining my reasons for dressing up.

Old man Jongilanga would not let me get away with it, though. "Is there any special reason for dressing up so well, my son?"

"Not any major reason, old man." I hesitated for a moment, and then decided to tell him. "I spent time with my wife and children this afternoon."

"That is good news, my son. I trust that this will lead up to them coming back to their home." The old man probably did not know that he was expressing my exact sentiments. If I could, I would make them come back home that very moment.

"I hope so too, old man," I said, sipping my tea. I didn't want to explain much. I was subjected to morality lessons for the rest of the afternoon.

"Family is very important, my son."

"Yes, old man. It's very important."

"You must guard the unity of your family with your life."

"I hear you, old man."

"There are so many things that cut lives short these days."

"Many things, old man."

"There is this disease that's ravaging young people."

"It's killing them, old man." I felt a pang of guilt cut across my chest as I uttered these words. The thought of the disease and its mysteries weighed me down. My estranged daughter, Nosipho, remains the only person I know for sure who has died of it. Many other people are rumoured to have suffered it, but they never admit publicly. I am still haunted by my own situation – thinking of my third test result, which is taking so long to arrive.

"We are running out of young people, my son."

"Young people are getting finished, old man."

"It is the things that they do these days that bring about these kinds of diseases."

"What do young people do, old man?" I asked, knowing that old man had strong views about the behaviour of the young people of today.

"Things that we see in the streets are shocking, my son." He started complaining about the youth of today who made a public display of their affections. "Look at my beautiful wife here," he said pointing at his wife, whose beauty had long since sunk in the furrows of wrinkles that criss-crossed her face. "We have half a dozen children together, but my lips, these thick lips, have never touched hers once!"

"You have never kissed her, old man?" I found myself thinking aloud. The old man's wife stared at him and shook her head.

"You say big things in front of children, Father," she mumbled and disappeared into the bedroom. The hinges of the bedroom door screeched as she closed it behind her.

"Never, my son. But I love her with all my heart. The children of today are always smooching each other on the street corners. What has happened to respect?"

"It's gone, old man. Respect is gone." By now I felt that the old man was stuck at a still point while the world around him was changing rapidly. Just that afternoon, I had felt like kissing my wife at the park for all to see.

When I had to go, old man Jongilanga asked his wife to iron his suit for him. It was the same brown suit that he had worn at Nosipho's funeral.

"What are you putting a suit on for, old man? Are you going somewhere?" I wondered.

"Yes, I'm going somewhere. I'm walking you out."

"You don't need to put on a suit for that, old man."

"Yes I do. You want people to think that I am your piccaniny?"

After his wife finished ironing we went to my car, which was parked right in front of the house. We stood there for a few minutes while old man Jongilanga gave me final words of wisdom. We must have said our goodbyes at least ten times before the final one. I drove slowly to my house, reminiscing about the happenings of that day.

As soon as my house came into sight, I felt like retracing my steps. It was a grim reminder that I should not be alone in it. My wife should be there. My children ought to be there. I knew how it felt to have a family. I had felt it that very afternoon at the park.

Earlier that day, I had touched my wife's hand. I saw happiness in her smile. I felt the warmth in her heart. I felt more or less the same as I did on that fateful day when we walked from school as teenagers. Now it had a deeper and more profound meaning. Maybe back then it was just youthful infatuation. But what had happened now was much more significant. My love for her was stronger. Even sitting next to her at the park was something profoundly gratifying.

A mosquito sang from a distance.

The irritating sound drew closer. Before I knew it, the insect was squealing next to my ear. I slapped the air very hard and thought that I had finally committed murder. Only for the sound to re-emerge. I made it my mission to kill the damned insect. After several attempts, I gave myself a hot *klap*. I removed my palm from my cheek and rubbed my fingers together. I could feel some wetness with my thumb. I switched on the light and saw a stain on my hand. I had killed the mosquito. It felt like a great accomplishment. And now the silence in my house had been restored. It was deafening.

My cheek felt itchy. The mosquito had taken a bite before joining the ranks of its ancestors. I got up and went to the bathroom. I stood in front of the mirror to assess the damage done by the mosquito. As I stood in front of the mirror, I noticed something else. What I saw was the splitting image of my father. It could only mean one thing – I was not getting any younger. I went back to bed to lament the deplorable prospect of ageing.

It was hardly a minute then I heard the sound of squealing dogs outside my house. It was the mating season for Lily. I was not ready to have grand-puppies yet, so I got up and went to the kitchen. Armed with a broomstick, I swiftly opened the door and found the troublesome bullterrier from the AmaCethe clan busy sniffing under Lily's tail. Lily had her tail tightly tucked between her legs. I charged at the bullterrier with the broomstick and it made a dash through the gate, which I had left open earlier that day.

The bullterrier had been after Lily's tail for a while, and I could see that it was going to cause trouble. I kept chasing it away, but it was clear that it was not going to give up easily. The proverbial saying that a dog never ends where it once got a bone might not apply now. Bruno did not need to have it before he became obsessed. Smelling was enough to drive him mad. If Bruno was anything to go by, a dog never ends where it once smelled the Promised Land. Bruno was always sniffing around my yard like a night-watchman.

Yesterday, we celebrated my daughter's birthday. I woke up early in the morning and cleaned the yard. My wife arrived, trailed by a truck carrying a jumping castle. My yard was transformed into a playground. Skade was there to assist in setting up for the party. Now the trouble was that the gate would have to be left open. I told Skade about the dogs that were making my life difficult. It would not be a pretty sight if they came and mated in front of my children while we were busy with the party. Besides, the idea of Bruno as Lily's puppy-daddy did not go down well with me.

Skade, the innovative Skade, came with a master plan. "It's easy," he said confidently. "You see, dogs were romantic from time immemorial."

"What do you mean, Skade?"

"You must observe their behavioural patterns. Dogs don't just jump on each other's backs without first doing thorough foreplay."

"Foreplay? How do dogs do foreplay?"

"They sniff. Dogs sniff and lick the bitch's behind before the intercourse." What Skade was saying made sense. Only the previous night I had caught Bruno doing exactly that. I had just never interpreted it as foreplay. "And how does that help us stop them from mating?"

"You see," he explained, "when they start there and realise that it does not smell nice, they will leave it. You just have to smear something that dogs don't eat on her posterior."

"You mean something like alcohol?'

"No. We need something stronger than that. Your car uses diesel, right?"

"Yes. You think it will work?"

"Yeah! Diesel can pass for perfect contraceptives for dogs." So, while my wife and children were busy preparing for the party, we went behind the house and called Lily. Skade held Lily tightly around her neck while I knelt behind her and carefully applied the diesel underneath her tail. I applied enough so that Bruno would smell it miles away.

At that very moment I heard Thembi's voice saying, "Dad, what are you doing with Lily's behind?" I turned around slowly, and I must have looked like a dog that had been caught stealing eggs in a chicken-shed. Thembi was in company of friends whose parents probably had reservations about them coming to my house for a party in the first place.

"Darling," I said, trying to formulate an explanation that might come close to making sense, "I'm applying diesel to make her strong."

"Can diesel also make me strong?"

"No, my child. Only dogs. It kills fleas, and a dog with too many fleas cannot be strong." At that point, I realised that it was time for us to leave Lily alone.

A short time later, I found myself in an even more difficult situation. While we were busy with the party, kids jumping up and down, pop blaring from the music system, and drinks flowing among the adults, the dogs were also busy. And not just cleaning the bones that were thrown away carelessly after the meat was removed. Let me just say, Skade's plan did work – but only for a short while. Suddenly I heard Thembi saying, "Dad! Lily ran out of diesel and now Bruno is pulling her." What Thembi witnessed was quite devastating to a father who was trying to rebuild a relationship with his children.

"What?" I came running, to be confronted by a sight I had once enjoyed when I was young. Bruno and Lily were locked onto one other. As young boys, we would beat the dogs until the horny bugger pulled out of the poor bitch.

"Sweetheart, please get inside because Lily gets shy when you look at her when she is being pulled." I waved Lily and her prospective puppy-daddy out of my yard. The children were left with their mouths agape. The gossipmongers would never stop talking about the bitch with diesel on the posterior.

The revellers started disappearing with their children. Sweet-wrappers, bones and empty bottles were the only remnants of all the life there had been earlier that day. At that point, Thuli probably realised that I needed some talking to.

"Can we talk?" she said, and I knew I was in trouble. When she says "Can we talk?" I know it's not going to be a pleasant conversation, or even a two-way conversation.

"I'm sorry for exposing the children to that kind of stuff, Thuli. I really tried to keep the dogs away," I said feeling very embarrassed. I knew it was a huge setback in my efforts to get forgiveness.

"C'mon, why are you gonna apologise on behalf of dogs? Dogs went dog, that's all," she said, a smile gently spreading to the corners of her mouth.

"I'm glad you understand. Thank you for doing this for me, Thuli," I said, wishing I could do more to show my appreciation. For a moment, my house had become a home. I had become the father that I should be. I felt complete.

"No, thank *you*," she said, chuckling. "We really had a great time."

"I hope they did."

"I have one more thing to discuss with you," she said in a more serious tone.

"And that is?"

"You'll hear tomorrow. I'll be here to help you clean up."

"C'mon Thuli, you know I'll be thinking about this through the night."

"At least you'll have something to look forward to."

"Okay, please give me a clue. I hate it when my mind is all over."

"Just check under your pillow. I left something there for you." I had not even noticed her going to the bedroom. It would have been such a good coincidence if I had found her there.

I kissed Nozi – Thembi had already fallen asleep in the back seat of the car. Thuli started the car and lowered her window.

"Please don't forget about tomorrow, then," I said as my goodbye to her.

"I'm the one who said I'll be here, remember?" She

flashed a grin and I waved as they drove off.

As soon as the car disappeared from sight, I made strides to the bedroom. I lifted the pillow and there was a brown envelope. My fingers were shaking as I ripped it open in a very disorderly manner. The paper looked familiar. I could see the letterhead of Lancet Laboratories on the reverse side. My fingers were shivering as I unfolded the paper.

What I saw in that paper changed my life. The results for my HIV test exonerated me from any possibility of carrying the virus. I felt like I was being given another chance in life, the same way I gave a second chance to the mouse. Tears started streaming down my cheeks.

PART FOUR

African Delights

The Queen of the Highlanders

◆

WE WERE AT OUR CREATIVE best when we made her. We gave her big bright eyes. We looked for a sharp nose to adorn her plump face. We gave her bright white teeth, small lips and a pointed chin. When we finished the job, we put a mole on her left cheek to mark the completion of perfect beauty. In short, she remains our most beautiful creation. Even this is not enough to describe the goddess that we created in Zodwa.

We, the Down People, have a responsibility to guard our creations. We guide them through life. We are always there for our children, but sometimes they turn a deaf ear to us and stop believing in us, and when they do this, they often take the wrong path. Our child went down this dreaded road, and we could not save her because she shut us out.

Some people thought our child had no troubles of her own. She had both brains and beauty. At the tender age of twenty-four, she had been to the big schools, she drove pricey cars and lived in a big house. Of course, they didn't know she was a troubled soul. In reality, Zodwa had everything – and yet she had nothing.

It all started when she got sponsorship to go to big schools in the Land of Gold. We, the Down People, had foreseen the future prospects of our child. We had said that she would read many books and go to faraway lands. Her people from the village of Ntselamanzi, the Place of Waters, in Alice, rejoiced when she finished schooling.

She came from a family that never had the fortune of receiving formal education. A goat was slaughtered and a libation was poured for us to quench our thirst. And so we travelled with her to the Land of Gold. When she got there, she welcomed us at the big school, and we were with her throughout.

Things changed when she met Samson Mokoena, the head of the Highlanders Consortium, a construction company owned by former freedom fighters. The Land of Gold was soon to become the land of rot. This happened after our child was declared the best creation in all the big schools in the Land of Gold, in some competition for beauty. For that, she got many earthly possessions as prizes, all provided by the Highlanders Consortium. But she never invited us into the new house, a townhouse she was allowed to live in as part of her winnings. We were still trapped in the school where she had welcomed us on her arrival.

The real trouble lay in our child's interactions with Samson Mokoena. At first, these were merely business interludes, but soon she, as the Queen of the Highlanders, was turned into a commodity, a brand. She began to think, appear and live as they desired. We wanted her to remain a child of our own. But she didn't.

We were sent by the ancients to whisper to our child.

We sent different signals, but Zodwa ignored our pleas when we visited her in dreams. That's how she was raised, and that's how she used to communicate with us before. But now her work as the face of the consortium took all the time she had. She was seen on television, heard on radio, and read about in magazines and papers. From a distant eye, it would seem that everything was going well for her. But of course, she was the child of our own, we were closer to her than anybody else, and we knew things that no other being could know about her.

When things started to take a downward turn during her second year at the big school, we felt her misfortune deeply. Her term as the Queen of the Highlanders was coming to an end, and she discovered that she had failed her previous year's exams at the big school. Her bursary was going to be withdrawn and she could not continue studying. Her village of Ntselamanzi, the Place of Waters, was beckoning.

Our daughter refused to listen.

She had no regard for the waters any longer. In the past, right from birth until this point, an appeal to the waters always had favourable returns for her. We gave her the good marks at school she asked for, cleansed her womb regularly, got rid of the pig lice she caught from the girl of our neighbours, got her a bursary to study at the big school; without fail, answers to all her wishes rained down on her. But now she was refusing the waters! As her problems mounted, and while she deafened her ears to our calls, the devil incarnate that is Samson Mokoena crept into her life and seized it.

We were there. We tried to open our child's eyes.

She paid us no regard. She didn't want to share her troubles with us any more. Instead, she cried to Samson Mokoena, the man who would take her hand and lead her into the pit. We heard her saying to him, in a moment of helplessness, "My life is changing so fast, Mr Mokoena. I am losing everything I thought I had."

"Look, Zodwa, you are a wonderful girl. We can't discard you just like that after you have done so much for us." He sounded sympathetic, but we knew better than to believe the words he uttered with his mouth.

"I'm glad you mention it, because I still don't know how I'm gonna cope with this situation. The car will be gone, the townhouse will be gone, and I've flunked my courses."

"Don't worry, my sweetie. All I need is your co-operation."

"Co-operation? I don't like the sound of that."

"I hate to have to name things, Zodwa, but next month the car you drive returns to the consortium, the townhouse will have a new occupant…"

"All right, all right!" she said, cutting him short. "I get the picture and it's a frustrating one."

"You seem disturbed," we heard Mokoena saying. "Is this frustrating you?"

"What kind of a question is that? This situation can barely excite anyone. The worst thing is that I will have to go home. I won't be able to return to Joburg next year."

"Why would you prefer to live in some godforsaken village in the Eastern Cape?" Mokoena was persuading our child like a man approaching a hot meal.

"What choice do I have? My parents can't afford to pay for my studies." Our child's voice revealed a deep anxiety, and we didn't understand why this was the case. We had been there for her before; we were going to be with her in the future. But she had lost confidence in us.

"What would you say if I offered to buy you a new sports car and went on renting your townhouse for you?" Mokoena enticed our child, and because she no longer valued our advice, because she thought we were no longer relevant to her life, because she had become accustomed to her new lifestyle, she did not listen to her inner self. She allowed herself to be manipulated by Mokoena.

"This isn't free," she said, more to herself than to Mokoena. "What's the catch?"

"All you need to do is attend business meetings with me. I'm a shareholder at the Highlanders Consortium, but I'm establishing a new company, Mokoena Construction and Maintenance. I want you by my side as an associate. We can define your role later. For now, you'll do this and that, whenever the situation demands – presentations and stuff like that."

"Me making presentations at business meetings? You are joking, right?" said our child, a smile slowly spreading across her face. And we knew then we had lost her to Mokoena.

We, the Down People, have been here before.

We know that a snake only shows its split tongue when it is getting ready to strike. What began as kindness quickly became what Mokoena had planned all along, and what we knew would always come. At first, our child's role was to make presentations to potential clients for the new company, or simply to be present at such presentations. The clients were sometimes hard to convince, but her beauty softened them, and made them say, "This is promising." And so the tenders to maintain the stadiums for the 2010 Soccer World Cup started to pour in to Mokoena's company.

Our child was seen at golf estates, where negotiations for some of the deals were conceived and sealed. Seeing her next to Mokoena, the golfers, who didn't all play that well, but who golfed anyway, would flock around and ask mundane questions. We saw the instant erection of pyramids underneath their trousers. The more they all competed to meet with Mokoena, buying his attention and subsequently that of Zodwa, the more money he made. None of this was acknowledged as the dirt it was by those involved. Mokoena meanwhile accumulated enough wealth to take him through to the grave and resurrection.

We never approved of our child's matrimony to Mokoena. How could we, when our child decided to marry herself without the blessing of the waters? There was no union of the elders and the Down People of the two clans. We could not enter the homestead of the Mokoenas when their Down People didn't know us, and neither could we allow them in our waters. We could no longer reveal ourselves to our child whenever we wanted to. Our spirit lingered in the land of rot, gold and silver. We protected our child on the roads and in the places she went to, but not at home – where she needed us the most.

Our duty is to protect our creations and not to punish their enemies. Had we not been the Down People, we would have done something to eliminate Samson Mokoena. But our responsibilities do not include elimination. So we offered our child what she was missing – compassion, with the hope that this might redirect her to the waters of her birth and sanity.

This came to her in a way that she never expected. It was a Saturday morning, and we decided to cleanse her womb. It was not her regular time yet, and she had none of the necessary cloths that girls use to absorb the cleansing, so she had to pay a visit to the nearest shop. We sent her to the garage to meet Simba, the gift of compassion that we, the Down People, had found to be compatible with her.

Simba had come all the way from beyond the Limpopo. He was at the garage looking for piece-jobs alongside other seekers, most of whom were refugees from neighbouring countries. All heads turned as the black, sleek and shiny dolphin on wheels sailed into the garage. It was a warm cloudless day. Our child hid her pretty face behind big, dark sunglasses and a straw hat, but this enunciated more than it hid her beauty.

As you all know by now, Simba was not the bravest of men when it came to dealing with women. It would have been more so with our child. A beautiful woman frightens even the bravest of men. But something happened to him. He was overwhelmed by palpitations, and a strong sensation crawled through his body as our child walked past. He could not repress the movement of his lips: "Ma'am, the only thing that's more beautiful than your car is you," he heard himself saying.

Our child felt a shiver of excitement when she heard this compliment from a total stranger. But this was strangely sweet to her, because lately she had been feeling less and less beautiful. This was obviously on account of Mokoena, who, she had realised, had not the slightest appreciation of her brains and beauty.

"Thank you, dear." She was quite sincere, and said this with a wide smile. The fact that she had responded was enough to give Simba a certain status among his fellow job-seekers. They all watched as she walked out of the garage shop back to the car. She deliberately swayed her hips this way and that, and the job-seekers seethed with wild desire. Once she got to the car, Zodwa removed her sunglasses and waved at the job-seeking stranger: "Can you wash a car?"

"Yes, Ma'am. I can do all household duties, including garden work. In fact, I'm an IT technologist by qualification," Simba presented his unsolicited resumé to her.

"Okay, okay, hold on," she said, chuckling, "I only need you to wash my car for now."

"I'll be happy to do that, Ma'am," he said enthusiastically.

This was the beginning of Simba's weekend car-washing job at the Mokoenas, which soon extended to working in their garden. At this point, our child and Simba didn't know that they were destined to be together. Zodwa started looking forward to weekends and the pleasant company that they brought. There was a mystifying connection between them, which they both felt, but each tried to suppress the longing they felt for the other. It went far beyond what was permitted by the mistress-and-servant formula.

One day Simba made a remark that lifted up Zodwa's self-esteem, which had sunk to its lowest point after Mokoena had ignored her for weeks.

He said, "Excuse me, Ma'am?"

"Yes, Simba?"

"I don't know how to say this, but... Can you tell me from which stream you cleanse yourself?"

"What do you mean, which stream?"

"I mean, the smoothness of your skin tells me that there are special waters you wash your face with," he said.

The delight our child took in this praise was beyond measure, and the rewards were gratifying for Simba. To his pleasant surprise, his job as a gardener was to become permanent that day. Soon he would occupy the cottage in the back yard as the family handyman. Our child opened her heart to Simba, and he became more at ease about taking initiatives that delighted her.

On the anniversary of our child's day of arrival, Simba planned a special lunch at her favourite restaurant as a surprise for her.

Earlier in the day, our child had requested him to collect her ostrich-leather jacket from the dry-cleaners. The jacket was her favourite clothing item; she had bought it on her last trip to the lands over the seas and mountains, where our eyes could not see. She had sent it to be cleaned in case, by some miracle, her husband remembered her special day, and decided to take her out that evening. Simba had returned without the jacket, telling a story about the ladies at the dry-cleaners who wouldn't give him the jacket, despite the fact that he had the receipt.

She left the house in a fury, determined to give the

cleaners a piece of her mind, with Simba behind the wheel. When they got to Melrose Arch, Simba made a detour to her favourite restaurant, where he claimed they would meet the manager of the dry-cleaners. And there it was, their table decorated with the petals of red and white roses. He pulled out a chair and beckoned her to sit. The employees sounded like a swarm of bees as they sang the "Happy birthday" song for her.

As they ate their favourite foods and laughed together, we were there, watching with admiration.

After contemplating for a while, our child took Simba's hand into hers. Her fingers were slender and small. Her hand was tiny and warm. Her touch caused a rush of blood through his whole body. He could feel her warm breath close to his mouth. She breathed the same air as him. He breathed the same breath as her. Their heartbeats were in harmony. Their souls intertwined in a labyrinth of longing and desire. One slight movement forward, and his lips would touch hers. But Simba moved away.

"Would you, eh, would you like a refill?" he asked nervously, even though her glass was still half-full.

"But why, Simba?" Zodwa hissed in desperation. She had waited too long for this moment, and now Simba had pulled back. Until then, our child was convinced that this was by far her best birthday ever. "No, I just thought you might need a refill."

"I'm not talking about that. Why do you have to spoil my birthday like this?" She sounded almost like a nagging child.

"I'm sorry, I didn't mean to … hey, it's getting late. Should I get you a refill or do you want us to go? We must beat the peak-hour traffic, and I'm sure Mr Mokoena has plans for tonight. There must be a big surprise waiting for you."

"Yeah right," she said dismissively, "the greatest surprise would be him remembering my birthday."

"Mazou, please, he's not that bad. He'll do anything for you." Simba always made her heart melt when he called her that. "Mazou" was what her closest friends used to call our child at high school. But she didn't like it said in the same sentence as her husband's name, not by Simba anyway. She reached for her handbag underneath the table.

"Don't even think about it. I'm gonna pay. This is your day."

"Simba!" Our child exclaimed in pleasant shock. She did not understand why the man had to try this hard when she knew all about his finances, but at the same time she was impressed with his display of gentlemanly propensities.

"No!" He lifted his finger against her mouth. As he did so, erotic thoughts began playing in her head. She wished those tough fingers would caress her body. A very tall man, Simba had a dark ebony face adorned with sprinklings of short beard. He had thick eyebrows, big black eyes, and a flat nose with large nostrils. Even more than his face, Zodwa admired his body. He had broad shoulders and his chest was noticeably hairy and muscular.

"Simba, you don't earn much. I'm responsible for your pay, remember?"

He ignored her and waved at the waiter. The waiter came running and asked if he could be of any help. "Paradzayi, can we have the bill, please?" Simba spoke as if he knew the man from somewhere, even though he was just reading the name from the tag pinned to the man's chest. It dawned on Zodwa that among the reasons she was attracted to Simba was that he was intelligent, honest and respectful.

"Certainly, Sir," Paradzayi said and turned to leave. Then, as if something had struck his mind, he walked back to the table. "Sorry to disturb, Sir, but I would like to know how come you pronounce my name so well. Can you speak Shona, Sir?"

"I am Shona, but I grew up in Bulawayo. My name is Simbarashe, my friends call me Simba," he said, stretching his arm to greet. Zodwa watched with a smile, appreciating every gesture that Simba made. "I'm glad to meet you, Simba. I see you are doing well for yourself. When did you come this side?"

"I've been here for five years now. I'm an IT technician by qualification, but I've been doing all sorts of jobs," Simba explained.

"Same here. I was a teacher before the old man messed up the country. This is the best job I've gotten since coming here three years ago," Paradzayi said. He and Simba started reminiscing about Kuwadzana, Simba's township in Harare.

Zodwa realised that some onlookers might have noticed the way she was drooling over Simba. She took her handbag and cleared her throat. "Sorry, guys, I've got to go to the ladies," she said, getting up.

"Over there, Madam," Paradzayi said, pointing in the direction of the restrooms. As soon as she got to the ladies' room, our child opened her handbag and took out a small make-up box. Her handbag was fitted with a mirror inside and she preferred using this to the ones in the bathroom. She carefully applied red lipstick. Like an artist carving a sculpture, she ran her eyeliner around her eyes with precision.

It was now afternoon, and as our child got back to the table, she saw Simba tuck his phone into his shirt pocket. She wondered what he'd been doing with it. It was known to us that he had been sending a text message to Mokoena, reminding him about his young wife's birthday.

Simba wasn't sure how much of this manoeuvre our child had noticed, and it made him nervous beyond pretence. Besides, he couldn't find it in him to lie to her.

"I'm ready to roll, Mr Chitongo," she said, standing next to him.

"Did you have a good time, Mazou?"

"It was great…" she said, wanting to add that it would have been even better had he not spoiled it by pulling away during their earlier moment of communion. Simba looked at her suspiciously.

"What's the look for, Sir? This really was great, okay? If only … all right, it was just great." She flashed a mischievous smile.

"If only?" He didn't know what to suspect: did she know about the text message to Mokoena, or had he done something ungentlemanly earlier? He thought he'd done things by the book. Now he felt embarrassed.

"This was a perfect date, the least you could have done was to give me a peck on the cheek." She spoke nonchalantly, but he knew she was serious.

The lift arrived and he pressed P1, where he had parked the car. They got inside the lift and she looked him in the eye and smiled. There was a tense momentary silence in which they both wondered if this was the time to rectify the earlier mishap.

"Okay, do it right here!" she blurted out.

"What? You think I can't hold you?" He grabbed her hand as they got out of the lift.

"Kiss me," our child found the courage to say. They were now standing next to her car. Simba looked around and timidly went towards her. He aimed for her cheek, but somehow his thick lips had touched hers.

He could not look her in the eye afterwards. He was now even more nervous. He got into the driver's seat while

Zodwa was still standing outside the car. "Aren't you gonna open the door for the lady?" she said mockingly, enjoying his embarrassment. Opening the car door for her was one of the gentlemanly traits that he had rehearsed in preparation for the day, but now it had slipped from his mind. He mumbled apologies and got out of the car to open the passenger door.

As he reached the door, our child stood closer to him. Before he knew it, she was holding him by the waist, and they began kissing, now with both their eyes and their minds shut. They fumbled into the passenger seat. Her breasts were pressed tightly against his chest. He charged at her like a bull towards a matador. Sweat was gathering on him, and the smell of it made Zodwa want him even more.

"Your phone is ringing?"

"I can hear it," said our child, pushing forward.

"It could be Mr Mokoena."

"Damn it! When will you learn to focus, Simba? I can return the stupid call later." She was devastated when he dislodged himself for the second time, yet again at a crucial moment. And he made it worse by bringing in the name of Mokoena just as love was about to take off.

Turning from him, she opened her handbag in a rage. She looked at the screen of her mobile phone, which was reflecting her husband's name.

"Hallo!" she gasped.

"Hey, baby love! I hear it's your birthday today," Mokoena said.

"You hear it's my birthday! Aren't you supposed to know about it?"

"Yes, my sweetie, that's what I mean. I set a reminder and it went off just now."

"Okay, what are you gonna do about it, then?"

"We have a board meeting tonight, so I can't be with you. I'll probably get home at about eleven or so, and I have an early morning tomorrow. But no worries, sweetie, I've booked a full body massage for you at the Entabeni Spa." He was such a strange man, that husband of hers. What good did it serve them as a couple when, to celebrate her birthday, he arranged for her body to be touched by a stranger?

She decided to cut the call short. "Okay, I'll see if I'm up for it. Bye," she said, happy to get rid of Mokoena.

"Bye-bye, baby love."

She hated it when he called her that. She was now angry and disappointed. She turned to Simba with even more vigour and barked at him: "You told him!"

"What?" Simba was bewildered.

"You told Samson that it's my birthday today."

"Is that what he is saying?"

"Simba, I'm not stupid. I know this man, and I know you. He wouldn't remember my birthday, especially not at four in the afternoon. You told him." She took his mobile phone and scrolled through the "sent messages". "See, I knew it!" She threw the phone at him, then gave him her back, gazing out the window with an angry frown.

"I'm sorry. I thought it would be a good thing if he knew. I wanted to see you enjoying your day, that's all." She kept looking away, watching the slow-moving traffic. What he'd just said about ensuring her happiness on her special day gave her a shortness of breath.

Simba was anxious. He kept glancing at her, not sure if she was crying beneath her sunglasses. "I meant well. I wouldn't do anything to hurt you. I'm really sorry, Mazou," he kept muttering.

The traffic was moving slowly on Oxford road. Simba caught a glimpse of himself in the rear-view mirror, and his heart almost stopped when he saw red lipstick on his mouth. He surreptitiously wiped off the lipstick. He took another glance at her to check if her mood had changed. It hadn't, but his mind kept going back to what had just happened between them. It was like a long dream that would end with him dirtying his underwear.

Next to him was the most beautiful pair of legs he had ever seen. He couldn't believe that his lips had finally rubbed against hers. He wondered how such a beautiful woman could have ended up with an obese, heartless old man like Mokoena. He had wild visions of himself taking her away from Mokoena, marrying her and having beautiful children with her. He had watched numerous films where the beauty escapes an arranged marriage to a prince, flees with a poor but wise and impassioned lover, and they live together happily ever after. But those were fairy tales. This was real life, and he was faced with a real problem.

Our child, on the other hand, had a meeting of her own in her mind. She had been disappointed by the man that she liked and desired so much. For months, she had been stealing glimpses of chest-hair under his shirt, watching perspiration slide down his neck as he worked in the sun, admiring the flexing of the muscles in his arms. Now she felt he was selfish to deprive her of these longed-for pleasures.

The hectic Friday afternoon traffic passed in a blur. Zodwa was brought back to this world by the barking of their neighbour's dog. The stupid animal never tired of barking and chasing their car, to the extent of sometimes trying to bite the wheels.

"That was heavy traffic. Can you believe that the accident was on the other side of the road? It's the curious onlookers on our side that delayed the traffic," Simba was saying as he unbuckled his seatbelt.

"What are you talking about?"

"Didn't you see that chain accident of six cars? The Fiat Uno was squashed between those massive cars like a loaf of fresh bread under an armpit," Simba explained, but our child was already stomping towards the house. Simba sat in the car, dismayed and feeling dejected.

He wondered how she could stay angry at him for the whole two hours, while sitting in the same car with him. He took out his phone and went to "sent messages" to re-read the message that caused all the trouble. He wanted to throw the phone away, very far away. But that wouldn't help much, he thought to himself. Instead, he was going to go inside the house and apologise to Zodwa one more time. What would Mr Mokoena think if he found the atmosphere so awkward between them? He gave a deep sigh. As he was about to leave the car, he noticed that she had left her handbag behind.

He opened the kitchen door and walked along the passage, carrying the handbag. He could hear the melodious voice of the musician, Lira, singing a serenading tune, "Crush". The song was our child's favourite melody, and she had played it so often that Simba had grown fond of it, too. He knew that playing romantic music was her way of unwinding. The song was from the songstress's *Feel Good* album, a choice that suggested to Simba that she was trying to work on her emotions.

There was no answer when he knocked on her bedroom door. He stood, trying to hear if our child was coming towards the door. After a while he realised that he was listening to the song – it could have been written for him. He had wild visions of being the man the songstress desired, to the point of getting hypnotised. Still transfixed, he did not hear the door opening.

"Is that singing or croaking?" Zodwa asked, a smile playing at the corners of her mouth. Her emotions had clearly changed for the better. The warmth of her face was a huge relief to him.

"It's singing, of course. Don't I sing better than that dreadlocked fellow who bastardised your national anthem in France?" he asked, releasing a broad grin.

"For a moment I thought there was a tortured dog outside my bedroom door."

Her head was tilted to the side and her left arm rested on her waist. "I used to sing tenor in the school choir," he told her, grateful that the apology he had planned didn't seem needed any more.

"So, you think today's musicians started in a school choir? Think about Macy Gray, Bryan Adams, Oliver Mtukudzi or even Mandoza for that matter, all with their croaky voices. Do you think they ever sang in a school choir?" she teased.

Simba was still enjoying our child's sudden change of mood and the beauty that it brought to her face. She was now wearing silky black lingerie. The fresh smell of her cologne reminded him of the marvellous smell of his primary-school teacher, the first woman he had desired – although he kept this to himself. "I'm just happy to see your eyes brightening again."

Her eyes always reminded him of the young Winnie Mandela, yet another woman he admired for as long as he could remember. His wall at his university residence had been decorated with posters of Winnie in her youth. Of all the sacrifices that Nelson Mandela had made, to him the greatest and obviously the most absurd was to leave such a young and beautiful wife, choosing a prison cell instead for almost three decades. He wouldn't let such beauty out of his sight for a second. Not even for the freedom of the nation!

"You couldn't even look me in the eye earlier. You are such a wimp!"

"Beautiful women like you should never sulk. Here, I brought your handbag." He gave her the handbag.

"Thanks. I don't know how I forgot it. I am never separate from my handbag."

"Well, that's why I thought I should bring it immediately."

"Let's see if you didn't steal some of my valuables. Come inside." He did so, standing shyly next to the door. She closed the door and opened the handbag. Then he heard what sounded like sweet-papers being unwrapped. She said to him, "Here, this is what I've been keeping for you."

He had instant palpitations as our child handed him a pack of the plastic tubes that are used for protection these days. He didn't know how it started, but he found himself locked in a passionate kiss with her. She was unzipping his trousers, he was pulling the lingerie free over her head. He tripped as they both tried, hurriedly, to take his pants off. She was giggling naughtily, and he was beginning to sweat. Then they were rolling on the thick and soft carpet of the bedroom. He fumbled around her waist and she raised her hips to allow him to take off her silky underwear. For the first time, Simba noticed that our child was more voluptuous than she looked in her tight-fitting jeans. He entered her immediately and she screamed with ecstasy. He groaned helplessly. We ran away.

We cannot be there when our child is opening herself up for intimate digging. It is not our domain. Ours is to shut the world around our child so that the horizontally joined couple inhabits a universe of their own. We returned after Simba's explosive ejaculation. He got up immediately and looked for his clothes, which were scattered all over the room.

"Hey, come back here," our child said to him. He

thought it logical to give her a kiss after such a fierce bout of love-making. He went back and tried to kiss her. Our child pulled him by the arm and he fell on top of her. They kissed and embraced each other. With a contented grin across her face, she asked, "Why didn't you take me to bed?"

"I'm a visitor here." By now, he was lying beside her.

"Visitors don't devour what doesn't belong to them with so much force," Zodwa said.

"Hey, what if he finds us here?" asked Simba, eager to leave.

"That was great actually. I never had it on the floor before," said our child, kissing him as he tried to wriggle free. He wondered why she didn't seem to have even a bit of remorse after their adulterous act, however great an experience.

"Actually, you must get paid for this. You are a professional." She was now playing with Simba's chest hair. He pushed her hand at once and got up.

"I must go," he said, filled with a sense of accomplishment and fear at the same time. Mokoena was a distant memory during the time that he was intimately connected to our child. Now the man's ugly image was coming back to haunt Simba, and, like the coward he was becoming, he wanted to leave her to deal with it on her own.

"Simba, I thought we were together in this," said our child helplessly.

"This was a mistake, Mazou," said Simba.

We had crossed rivers and lakes to find him – our gift of compassion to our child. We had allowed him to reach the intimate depths of our child and drink from the waters of the ancients. He was one with Zodwa. He had become part of us.

We, the Down People, cannot destroy what we created.

African Delights

◆

We were there, watching.

It was 10 April 2010, exactly two months before the start of the biggest sports gathering in our land. Visitors from all over the world were expected to start streaming to our shores. Our child, Zodwa, was embarking on a new endeavour – establishing African Delights. This was the day it would be launched.

She was woken up by light beaming harshly through her eyelids. Mokoena had switched on the overhead light as opposed to the bedside lamp, although she always asked him not to. Why did everything she said to him seem to go through one ear and out the other? she wondered. This is not a good way to start a day, she chastened herself.

She tried to suppress a yawn, taking care not to let Mokoena notice that she was awake. She listened carefully. Neither his asthmatic breathing nor the shuffle of his gout-infected feet were audible. She opened her eyes slightly and looked around like a rabbit about to vacate its nest. Satisfied that she was alone in the bedroom, she stretched her arms and reached for the watch on his side of the bed. The time was 7:35, and she was sure to miss her first appointment of the morning. She was expected to be at Monty's Décor to prepare for that afternoon's function.

The launch of African Delights had taken weeks of intense preparations. She was no longer sure about this initiative. We had whispered to her that it was a morally despicable undertaking. Mokoena had told her that it was a lucrative business. Needless to say, at that time she found Mokoena's promise more appealing. Now our whispers were beginning to reverberate beyond her immediate world. But, instead of turning to us, she chose to look down at her feet, hoping that as she was going forward she wouldn't sink into contaminated waters.

She tried to get up, but only lifted her head for a moment. The magnetic pull of the pillow drew her back. She succumbed to the seductiveness of the bed and fell asleep instantly. She enjoyed taking these momentary naps in the morning. She would struggle to fall asleep throughout the night, but managed to catch a few short intervals of sleep when it was time to wake up. In spite of their brevity, the morning naps were deceptively enjoyable.

As she tried to catch up with her sleep, she could vaguely hear Mokoena speaking from a distance. The clink of plates in the sitting-room told her that Mokoena was having breakfast with someone. She identified the other voice as Simba's. A Zimbabwean émigré with a qualification in information technology, Simba first came to the house to wash her car, then became their gardener before becoming the household's handyman. He lived in a cottage in their back yard, which made him part of the family – to some extent. Their house attendant, as they preferred to call Maggie, the maid, lived in Alexandra Township and the efficiency of the public transport was never predictable.

This morning, our child decided to hibernate in bed until Mokoena left the house. She could not bear the sight of the man these days. She heard him release a huge belch, one of those loud explosions that come from deep down in the abdomen. She resented this bad habit of his, but she was very close to giving up on trying to reform him. If his mother had failed to teach him manners, who was she to think that she could teach an old man like Mokoena how to behave at the breakfast table? Then she heard him drag his feet towards the bedroom. She hastily drew the duvet over her head and pretended to be sleeping.

"Heh, Zodwa, come on, it's getting late. Wake up!" Mokoena said as he saw our child covered in a silky cream duvet. "This woman, do you know what today means? Zodwa, wake up!" he said shaking her by the shoulder.

"Hmm?" Our child winced and turned slowly to face Mokoena. Her eyes were slightly open, and she spoke softly, like the sick person she was pretending to be. Mokoena was still in his night robe, but he had already taken a shower. He had vowed never to use the bath again after it had shrunk significantly.

There had been a mortifying episode when he had been trapped in the bath, and had called on our child for help – but she did not possess enough power to pull him out. His potbellied body was wet, slippery and enormous. It was no different from trying to pull a hippo out of a river. Our child, a tiny former beauty queen, stood no chance. Simba was called in to assist. They each held him by one arm, and it was only then that they were able to rescue the naked man. Simba was sworn to secrecy, and no one dared to mention this incident.

"Wake up!" Now he shouted at our child as she pretended to doze.

"C'mon, Samson, it's still early and I need to rest a little bit," she said in a sluggish voice. "Headache is killing me."

"Why don't you just get pain block or something?"

"No, I'll put down for a few more minutes."

"I don't want anything going wrong when Comrade TK gets here, you hear me?"

"I know, okay? I'm just not feeling well, that's all."

"Okay," he said, taking off his robe and putting on a

shirt. He then picked up the bedroom handset to make a call on the intercom. "Simba, please come!" A minute later Simba entered the room. He had been anticipating the call, which came every morning.

"This pair, Sir?" Simba asked.

"Yes, that one, Simba. Can't you see the pants that I'm gonna wear?" said Samson, pointing at a pair of trousers on a hanger. "They match, Simba. You must not just wear anything. Your clothing must match."

"Yes, Sir." Simba knelt in front of his employer and first put the socks onto his feet. Then he struggled with the shoes. Samson's feet kept on swelling like they were made of self-raising flour. This did not make it easy for him to put on shoes. Simba was assigned the duty of assisting Samson every morning, putting on his socks and shoes for him, and tucking his shirt into his pants. In fact, it was not so much the shirt as the belly that Simba had to thrust inside the trousers every day.

"Okay, now get my briefcase and put it in the car," ordered Samson. He took one last look at our child and saw that she was fast asleep. He shook his head without saying anything.

"And, Simba," he turned as if remembering something important, "don't forget that Comrade TK arrives at two o'clock. Okay?"

"Yes, I won't forget, Sir," Simba affirmed, wondering why he had to be reminded about the same thing again and again.

"And tell Maggie to sleep over tonight. We don't know what time the function will end."

"I have already told her, Sir. She will also bring clothes to change into."

"Good. I'll be back at twelve, and the function starts at two. All right?"

"It's fine, Sir."

"Good. Now I'm off to headquarters. I'm sure some other comrades from the meeting would be interested in attending the party. We must have enough champagne and single-malt, all right?" he said, struggling to adjust the seat of his car. His enormous Chrysler C300 tilted to one side as he wedged himself into the driver's seat.

We, the Down People, we protect our creations.

Our child was relieved that Samson had finally left. She was beginning to see the light. We tried to show her that the man was not good for her. He never showed any respect for her. Their relationship, which subsequently led to marriage, was instigated by his ex-wife, Makgotso, who had the audacity to call on the phone and insult our child, calling her a whore.

The gossip streams had flowed in the direction of the wife of Mokoena. She did not take kindly to the news that Samson was busy frolicking with a young beauty queen, courting the affections of our child. Apparently she, the rightful wife of the Mokoenas, kept receiving papers from the bank for a car that her husband did not drive. What followed were traffic fines issued at awkward hours and in areas that she did not think her husband even knew about. She made it her business to find out who this young mistress was. She called the traffic department, and after some persuasion, she got the phone number of the regular driver of the car. She immediately dialled the number, using Samson's phone.

"Hello, dear," our child answered in a lively voice. The caller went quiet, but she could not hide her heavy breathing, something that startled our child.

"Samson, what's wrong? Are you okay, my love?" our child enquired.

"You whore, you are calling my husband your love!"

Mrs Mokoena blurted out the expletives.

"I'm sorry, I…" Zodwa was so devastated, she couldn't even respond to the name the woman had just called.

"What are you sorry for, screwing my husband? You lured my husband into buying you a car. You parasite!"

Our child could not bear the insults any longer. We could not listen to them either. We whispered to our child that she should hang up the phone. A minute later, the phone rang again. Zodwa was wise enough to listen to us and ignored it. The phone rang until the call was forwarded to voice mail. After a while, a text message came through. Our child regretted reading it because she felt that it pierced more deeply and painfully than the verbal insults. The message read: *I trust that it's only money that you are after; that's the reason I'm still in this marriage too. Just don't give Aids to Samson because a whore like you probably has tons of it.*

Our duty is to protect our creations. Their tribulations are ours.

Our child was troubled. We were there when she swore to her last drop of blood that she would take him of the Mokoenas away from the old woman. She was too angry, too resolved, to listen to our protestations. And Mokoena was a willing victim. He was never averse to the idea of a divorce. His only concern was the amount of wealth he stood to relinquish in the process.

There was a promise of good things to come for Mokoena. His comrade from Robben Island and then exile, Toxic Komanisi, popularly known as Comrade TK, had returned to politics to become the Minister of Reconstruction and Development. TK had been in business for close to ten years. During that period, he amassed so much wealth that his ministerial salary was a significant downgrade. But he was a great visionary, and had the necessary charm to enhance his political ambitions. His strategy was to keep his friends close, the President's faithful supporters closer, and to project himself as the voice of reason in a rather debilitated movement. With the suppression of credible leaders in the movement, populism was becoming the trendy way to scale the political ladder.

Although publicly he appeared to be cuddling the President, TK was always ready to pounce into the presidential boots if the President stumbled. He knew with perverse certainty that there would come a time when the President would fall from grace.

We had seen it happen before. We, the Down People, are the voices of the ancients.

We leaped into the future and saw that Mokoena would prove to be a danger to our child. We whispered to her to stay away from Mokoena. We were watching as he started transferring copious amounts of money into her account, sold some of his assets, and then filed for divorce. Makgotso was quite happy with the divorce settlement, although it was relatively small, considering Mokoena's riches. And so Mokoena went ahead and married Zodwa without our consent, or that of the elders from the Place of Waters. The voices of the ancients were muted. Our child had stopped listening to her inner self.

We are of the waters. When a fish takes a leap out of the waters, it has to drop back in. And when it ignores the call of the ancients to come back into the waters, it will be found floating on the surface. Lifeless.

It was sad to see our child moving further and further away from the waters. Together with Mokoena, she established African Delights. Mokoena explained it as a multipurpose hospitality agency whose purpose was to "provide everything that a human heart desires". Our child became the Chief Executive Officer and Mokoena the Owner and Managing Director of the company. The way it worked, Mokoena would legally own the company, while our child would run it on a day-to-day basis.

This day, 10 April 2010, Mokoena got home an hour earlier than he had promised.

"Simba, where is this woman?" That's how this Mokoena referred to our child – this woman.

"She went to get the flyers, Sir," replied Simba, the man we had chosen for her.

"And that can take this long?" Mokoena said, exasperated.

"She'll also pick up some models on her way back, Sir."

"But doesn't she know we are hosting Comrade TK today?"

"Yes, she knows, Sir. But you said she must be here by midday. It's an hour earlier now," Simba explained.

"Stop arguing with me, just call her and tell her that she must come home now."

"Yes, Sir." Simba took his mobile phone and went to the balcony to make the call.

"Mazou, where are you?" Simba enquired as soon as our child answered her phone.

"Is he already asking for me?" she asked, and before Simba could respond, she went ahead, "He must relax, okay."

"But you know he's really anxious about today. Apparently this TK guy is someone big."

"I know, I know, just tell him that I'm on the way. I'll be there in twenty minutes."

"Please be here in twenty minutes, then. Bye." Simba went back inside, where he found Mokoena pacing up and down the corridor, glancing at his wristwatch and looking through the glass door of his living room, as if he was anticipating someone to emerge on the other side.

The intercom rang and Mokoena jumped to answer it.

"Hallo?" he answered.

"Good morning, Sir."

"Who's this?" Mokoena asked.

"We are Jehovah's Witnesses," the caller said.

"To hell with Jehovah's Witnesses!" Mokoena smashed the handset down.

"Who was that, Sir?" Simba inquired.

"Bloody Jehovah's Witnesses."

"But you said they must go to hell."

"Yes, those hypocrites deserve burning in hell."

"Sir, Jehovah's Witnesses belong in heaven, not hell."

"Well, this is not their heaven. What is this woman saying now?"

"She's on the way, Sir."

"Good. Now, let's make sure that everything is ready. Are there enough supplies: food, meat, alcohol?"

"Yes, there should be enough, Sir."

The intercom rang again, "What is it?" he answered angrily.

"Sorry?" we heard an elderly voice saying.

"Oh, it's you, Maggie. Come inside, please." He pressed the button and the electric gate opened. Maggie entered through the kitchen door.

Maggie was herself a messenger of her own Down People. She understood the language of the ancients and cherished their existence.

She put her still-dripping umbrella behind the door. She took off the plastic bag that she put on to cover her head from the drizzle. Her maroon woollen beret emerged safe and dry from beneath the plastic bag. She took off her black raincoat. She wore a brown jacket and a floral dress underneath the raincoat. The dress was her best, but the jacket rarely came off her back. She even wore it to church on Sundays. She hung it behind the door. She wiped her thick glasses against her woollen jersey and put them on again. She opened her handbag and took out a bundle of green wool and knitting needles, along with a piece of knitted fabric. Whenever anyone asked, she said it was a jersey she was knitting for her grandchild. She had been knitting it for the past three months, but nothing in its current form resembled a jersey or anything that could be worn.

She took her overall, which hung behind the kitchen door. Maggie continued leaving her overall behind the door despite Zodwa's protestations. Our child thought doing so was untidy, while Maggie felt that it was convenient. In the end, Maggie's opinion prevailed. She put on the overall, and then turned to this side and that, looking at her waist. She was a round-figured woman with an ample bosom. Satisfied with her appearance, she walked to the living room where Mokoena and Simba were.

"Hey, Maggie, I've been worried about you. I thought you might forget to come to work," said Mokoena.

"No, I couldn't forget, Sir. It's just that there is a taxi strike, so I had to wait for the train today."

"Taxi strike, what is it now? I hope they don't start shooting each other again."

"The taxi drivers are protesting against the BRT system."

"The BRT system?"

"Yes, these new buses that have been brought by the white man."

"Oh, you mean the Bus Rapid Transport. What is the problem now?"

"They say something about the BRT propating their intelligent property," Maggie explained.

"You mean they are appropriating their intellectual property?'

"Something like that," she said.

"I don't understand." Mokoena was looking at her quizzically.

"They say the transport routes that the BRT is using were invented by the taxi drivers."

"I see, maybe I should investigate this BRT thing. There might be a business opportunity right there," Mokoena said thoughtfully.

"Okay, let me change and get ready, Sir."

"Why are you wet? Has it started raining outside?"

"No, it's just a fly's spittle," Maggie said.

"That fly's spittle is gonna ruin my plans! My guests won't be able to sit outside to watch the models in swimming costumes. This is supposed to be a pool party."

"Pool party?" Maggie was astounded.

"Yes, Maggie," Mokoena said dismissively. "Now, can you dish out for us, please? We must eat before the guests start streaming in."

"Okay, Sir." Maggie realised that Mokoena didn't want her to ask too much.

"Sir, I have never seen you using the swimming pool before. Why would you host a pool party at the end of autumn?" Simba asked because the memory of Mokoena trapped in the bath was still very fresh in his mind, although he knew better than to refer to this incident.

"C'mon, Simba, you know I don't give a damn about swimming! It's all about the display. The waitresses today will be beauty queens in swimming costumes. Hah, Simba, you know nothing. Today is the day."

Maggie entered with a tray of food. She put it in front of Mokoena and removed the cover. As clumsy as she was in other areas, Maggie had a special way of preparing beef stew. She dipped a spoon and took a bite. She then took a piece of beef, chewed and swallowed it. "Thank you,

Maggie," Mokoena said with satisfaction as she went back to the kitchen.

"Why does she take a bite of your food before giving it to you?" Simba finally gathered courage to ask, having observed this ritual many times.

"You can never be too safe, Simba. Women kill their husbands these days. I'm not taking chances, not even with Maggie here, because Zodwa might pay her to put poison in my food. Never trust a woman!"

That's what he thought of our child – that she wanted to kill him. They lived under the same roof, and yet they didn't live together.

"Now, about this afternoon, do we have everything?"

"I believe so."

"Simba, don't believe! You must make sure that you stock a variety of single-malt whiskeys. I met with Tom Myekeni at the headquarters. He'll be coming with a group of Tender Kids today. You know they are the future of our movement. And they like their whiskey, those boys."

The Tender Kids were the youth component of the governing party. Like all youth formations, they were radical in their outlook. Unlike their predecessors who had been young intellectuals with dynamic political minds, the Tender Kids often equated radicalism with ill-discipline. They insulted monarchs, bishops and incumbent presidents, all in the name of radicalism. The reason Mokoena liked them was because they were the proponents of economic empowerment. To some of them, empowerment meant that young people who could barely wipe their bums had to be given large amounts of money to build roads, bridges and houses that disintegrated even before they were finished.

"Sir, does Comrade TK drink anything special?"

"Simba, Comrade TK is a man of class. He loves his Moët & Chandon. He won't settle for anything less. He owns a wine estate in the Cape winelands. You can't fool him. That guy knows his wine." As Mokoena spoke, bits of food flew out his mouth like water out of a sprinkler.

"How come he is known as Comrade TK?"

"His name in full is Toxic Komanisi. We gave it to him as a combat name in exile. He is a true communist."

"So you've known him for a long time," Simba said as he wiped the last bit of gravy on his plate.

"*Hawu*, Simba, Comrade TK and I go a long way back. We kept the communist ideology alive in exile. Come to my study, I'll show you." As they got to the study, Simba was struck by the collage of photographs that lined the walls. There was a shelf filled with moth-eaten books with yellowing pages. He could see titles like *The Communist Manifesto* by Karl Marx, *Animal Farm* by George Orwell, *Wretched of the Earth* by Frantz Fanon, and several books on Fidel Castro, Kwame Nkrumah and other revolutionaries. The thick dust on the shelves told Simba that the books had not been opened in a while.

"You see, this was when we got to exile in 1976. I skipped the country after my release from the Island," Mokoena said as he took Simba through the pictorial odyssey of the liberation movement.

"But you were so small."

"I didn't ask you to comment on my weight, Simba. Do you want to hear about these pictures or not?"

"I'm sorry, Sir," Simba apologised. "So, what is Comrade TK doing here today?

"We talk business, Simba. I'm gonna make money. You hear me? Real money," said Mokoena, rubbing his fingers together.

"But I thought you already have enough money, Sir."

"Enough, did you say enough? Simba, clearly you don't know where I come from. I lived in exile for almost twenty years. When we came back, I had to start from scratch with nothing. Absolutely nothing!"

"And how did you accumulate so much wealth in such a short time, then?"

"Simba, you wouldn't believe what I went through. I had this typewriter and I had to do something with it. I couldn't think about being a writer because we all know that artists starve to death. So I started typing out programmes for funerals."

"You mean you made money out of that?" Simba was perplexed.

"That is how I opened my first printing business, Sam's Printers. There's always a funeral every weekend, Simba. I made enough money to survive out of those programmes. But I did not get involved in the struggle in order to survive. I had to acquire my fair share of the country's wealth. So I formed the Highlanders Consortium with three other comrades. We had to rebuild the country. People had to get housing," Mokoena argued.

"But up to this day housing remains a problem – after sixteen years!"

"Rome was never built in one day, Simba."

Simba found it fascinating that Mokoena could quote something so convenient. Wasn't it ironic that an individual's wealth could accumulate in just sixteen years, and yet the same number of years was not enough to rebuild a country? Simba wanted to ask, but decided against it.

"Now, Simba, with this one, the African Delights, I am on my own. I don't need to split the cheque four ways."

"I didn't think that the hospitality industry paid that much."

"Simba, this is the most sustainable business you can ever think of. We'll start off well with the Soccer World Cup visitors. Our target markets are the sex-starved businessmen, the ever-travelling politicians and tourists, especially those who'll be attending the Soccer World Cup."

At that moment, our child arrived with three slim girls in her vehicle. She was followed by a bigger vehicle, filled with about ten young girls. We saw them sporting cloths that only just managed to cover their genitals.

"Yah, that's what I'm talking about!" Mokoena said as he saw them getting out of the car and heading for the pool-side. "No man in his right mind will be able to resist these beauties."

"And where will those women operate from?" enquired Simba.

"Simba, you think I am going to turn my house into some cheap brothel? C'mon, you know me better than that. Tourists will decide what kind of women they want, and where they want to meet them."

"How will they know which woman is available?"

"We have the portfolios of the models on the website. We've got all kinds of flavours – chocolate-brown Indians, smooth-skinned Chinese, peroxide blondes, brunettes, Africans with wide hips and round buttocks. Even Brazilian girls with vivacious bodies and smooth long legs. You see, Simba, all they have to do is click the button. We'll do the bookings, and they'll pay for the flights of the women, rent them hotels. Whatever happens there is none of my business. I am not a pimp; I'm just a businessman."

"And how does this all relate to the World Cup?"

"That's my consumer base. Any country that needs cheer ladies can come here; any player, administrator or fan who needs special treatment can just contact African Delights; we'll give them the time of their miserable lives. We'll take them to the depths of Africa and her beauty."

At that moment, the bell rang. "Hey, Simba, I can't

believe it's almost time. I hope that's Comrade TK. He was not in the meeting this morning," said Mokoena, picking up the receiver to answer.

"Hallo, welcome to African Delights. How can I help you?"

"Bra Sam, it's Spoiler of the Tender Kids. Has the party started yet?"

"Spoiler, please come inside. We are about to start," said a delighted Mokoena, pressing the button to open the gate. A convoy of four luxurious cars glided into the yard, led by a red Aston Martin. Tom Myekeni parked his flamboyant red Bentley in the driveway, where all the guests were sure to pass. It had a personalised Tomi 2 GP numberplate, and everyone knew to whom it belonged.

"Hey, welcome gentlemen," Mokoena said, opening his arms to receive the entourage of Tender Kids. Their dress sense suggested that they had escaped from a lunatic asylum. Half a dozen of them wore expensive floral shirts, shiny suits with tight-fitting pants and sharp-pointed shoes. Those who were always on the wrong side of the wheel, no matter which way it turned, scornfully referred to that type of shoes as "tender shoes". The long noses, they argued, were meant for sniffing out the direction of government tenders. Hence every advertised tender always fell into the lap of some politically connected individual, regardless of their lack of expertise in the specified field.

More guests started pouring in, including the top brass of the ruling party. Spoiler already had a green bottle in his hand.

"Thank you for inviting us, Bra Sam," Spoiler said. Our child walked towards them wearing a broad smile.

"Who's this chick, Bra Sam?" Spoiler asked with eagerness.

"Sorry to interrupt," our child said, good-humouredly,

"I just wanted to welcome our guests." No matter how long she had been out of the waters, regardless of how much she tried not to listen to us, the voices of the ancients were still embedded deep down in her. She was never disrespectful, this child of ours.

"Zodwa, please meet Spoiler Mangena, the leader of the Tender Kids. Spoiler, this is my wife, Zodwa." Spoiler was dumbfounded for a moment. Our child's beauty had that effect on young men like him.

"Nice to meet you, Spoiler," said our child, stretching her hand to greet.

"Likewise. Do you have a sister?" Spoiler asked as he held onto our child's hand for longer than was necessary.

"Eh, Zodwa, can you make sure that Spoiler, Comrade Tom and the rest of the Tender Kids are served drinks? What would you guys like?" Mokoena intervened, noticing that the young men were drooling over his equally young wife. It was clear that they could not suppress their simmering appetites and, like the children that they were, he had to put a bottle in their mouths to stop them making noise.

"Any single-malt whiskey will do for me," Spoiler said.

"Me, I don't commit statutory rape. I only drink whiskey that's eighteen years or older," Tom said, to uproarious laughter.

"All right, come this way, gentlemen. The party is actually down by the pool-side." Mokoena began ushering his guests to the back of the house.

"Wow, I think I love this place already," we heard Tom Myekeni say as he saw a waitress clad in a green-and-yellow bikini. She stood posing with her left hand on her hip. In her right hand, she held a tray with bits of calamari, sushi, biltong and other small snacks. Behind her was another one in a similar pose and dress, but serving champagne and whiskey. Mokoena moved to the makeshift podium and asked for the attention of the guests.

"Thank you, ladies and gentlemen, our guest speaker has arrived."

There were cheers as the guests acknowledged the presence of their leader, Comrade TK. Even the unruly Tender Kids were quiet when TK took to the podium.

"*Amandla*!" Comrade TK greeted the participants in the revolutionary fashion of shouting power to the people.

"*Ngawethu*!" The guests responded unanimously. The power is ours. A tall and handsome man, TK had a presence. His booming voice was hard to ignore. He had a good command of English language and chose his words carefully.

After apologising for his late arrival, which was due to an urgent business meeting, TK commended his old comrade, Mr Samson Mokoena, for being such a visionary and astute businessman. "Good businessmen are those who are forward-thinking. Those who know what the needs of their clients are even before the clients realise it themselves," he said, to loud cheers from the guests. Mokoena kept nodding, acknowledging the kind words that came from his comrade.

After Comrade TK's speech, which did not feel long, even though he spoke for well over twenty minutes, Mokoena handed him a pair of scissors to cut the ribbon. TK cut the ribbon with ease, smiling for the cameras as he performed the ritual. He drew aside a curtain to unveil a plaque. The words "African Delights" were written in gold, and below them was the image of a semi-nude woman reclining on what looked like a beach. TK read the inscription below the image aloud, to loud cheers: "We provide everything that a human heart desires."

We were there, watching.

We saw Mokoena shaking hands with TK. He handed him an envelope that contained a voucher for African Delights. We heard him telling TK to choose any kind of entertainment he wanted for that night. We were also watching when Tom Myekeni was called on to propose a toast. The champagne popped open before he could say a word. He announced that the popular local artist, Sizzler, and her dance group, were about to astound the guests with a performance. Sizzler had a trick of selecting a man from the audience, gyrating with him on stage, and leaving the rest of the men drooling and running amok.

Sizzler's performance was followed by more champagne pops, cheers and ululations from the guests. Mokoena walked over to TK, who was now talking to one of the models. He hesitated for a moment, waiting for the honourable guest to finish his conversation with the girl. Realising that the conversation was taking longer than he expected, he stood next to the two and cleared his throat in an attempt to attract Comrade TK's attention. The girl noticed him and flashed an even-toothed grin. Her skin was strewn with goosebumps.

"Hey you," Maggie called to the model. "Are you feeling the cold?" We cheered Maggie on. She was our only hope for salvation.

"No, I'm fine, *Mme*." The girl could not explain that she was at work, and that they were required to wear almost invisible bikinis.

"Come now, my child," Maggie said, taking off her brown jacket and handing it over to the model. "Put this on. I can't keep warm when a little undernourished girl like you is cold." The girl obligingly took the jacket.

"Maggie," shouted Mokoena, appalled. "Please leave these girls alone. Can't you see that they are wearing uniform?"

"You mean nudity is their uniform?" Maggie was astonished.

"Maggie," Mokoena realised that this was not going to be easy. "Please come this side. I want to speak to you before we finish here."

We watched him as he took the jacket from the model and went with Maggie back to the house. Maggie kept turning to look at the half-naked girls who stood like street lamps in the rain, waiting to serve food to potbellied men with moon-shaped faces. What Maggie did not realise was that she was seeing a growing trend in the South African society. Rich men displayed their wealth by splashing out on parties where young girls were reduced to ornaments and troughs for the men's amusement.

"Maggie, you've been working hard these past few months," Mokoena said as soon as they got into the house. "I want you to take leave, starting today." Maggie protested that she did not need the leave, but Mokoena insisted, saying that Maggie was not "a Mokoena slave". She deserved a break. He then called Simba to take Maggie to the taxi rank.

The rain started pouring down more heavily. There was a stampede of guests as they hastily moved under the marquee. Mokoena's eyes darted from corner to corner, trying to locate his guest of honour. He saw TK on the balcony, chatting to a different but equally beautiful girl to the one he had previously been talking to. He walked over to TK and stretched out his arm. "I really thank you for coming, Comrade TK," Mokoena said as he shook hands with his guest speaker. "No, thank *you* for introducing the concept. And especially for the voucher," said TK, caressing the girl next to him. She was now wearing his jacket over her bikini.

"Are you using it already?" Mokoena asked, with

a mischievous smug across his face. "This is gonna be a delightful evening," we heard TK saying as he walked to his German sedan with his prize in tow.

We looked for our child. She was not by the pool-side. She was not part of the celebrations. We saw her through the window. She was sitting on her bed, crying. But she never called upon us to intervene.

The Best of African Delights

◆

WE ARE CLOUD GATHERERS.

We collect waters burned by the sun on the ground and help them rise to the highest skies. But when the One Who Appeared First decides to release a drop of rain from the skies, we open our hands and welcome it back to the community of waters on the ground. For His decision cannot be overturned.

Our child was devastated. Her whole body shivered. We don't usually wrestle with our creation, but that day we had to come out of the waters to prevent Zodwa from responding to the message. We wanted her to ignore it. We held her thumb in midair. She saw it shaking like a lone leaf dangling from a naked tree. She closed her eyes, bit her lower lip and heaved a deep sigh. Then she opened her eyes and went back to the message from Baer Schweinesteiger. She read it once more and felt anger welling up in her chest.

Schweinesteiger, the big man from the world federation of the ball, was bringing a large delegation to our soil. Our child knew him well: he had been a regular client with African Delights since its establishment. He had come to our soil many times before, and he loved the variety of African dishes on offer at African Delights. His preference was for an African Delight that was chocolate-brown, vivacious and long-legged. He was obsessed with African women's bums: they had to be round and protruding, like the three-legged African pot. Those were his specifications, and our child always went out of her way to recruit new "entertainers" for him. She was presently expecting a new contingent of trainees from Thailand, Portugal and Brazil via Mozambique.

But now Schweinesteiger had sent a specific request that had left our child dumbfounded. Each time she read his message, her heart knocked vigorously in her chest: *"Dear Zodwa, I want the best of African Delights. I want you."*

Our child never thought Schweinesteiger would ever make such an incongruous request. He knew that Zodwa was a married woman. He also knew that Samson, with whom he had business dealings, was her husband. But the message was not a mistake. It had her name on it.

Our child had to tell her husband about it. She found him in his study, with a spreadsheet laid out on his desk. He had a calculator in his hand and was working frantically on his figures.

"What are you busy with?" our child asked, gently placing her hands on his shoulders.

"What a businessman should be busy with," Mokoena said, without looking at our child.

"And that is?" She bent forward, looking over his shoulder and saw headings such as "Entertainment for Opening Ceremony", "Guided Tours for the Executive Committee", "Stadium Maintenance after World Cup", and so on. Under each heading were financial projections. The man was budgeting for the World Cup projects, our child concluded.

"Baby love, Mr Schweinesteiger is arriving with the delegation tomorrow. I'm working because we must finalise everything by Sunday."

"Actually, I want us to talk about him," our child said.

"What about him? Can't it wait until I finish with my budget here?"

"I would do away with that budget, if I were you. Those

business deals might just fall through if you knew what he was up to now." We were glad to hear our child talking like this. It was a reminder that she was still a child of our own.

"What do you mean?" asked Samson, turning to face his wife and pushing his glasses up the bridge of his flat nose. "What could possibly disrupt my business deals with Schweinesteiger? This is a critical moment for me," he said, growing furious.

"That man is a pervert! Can you believe that he wants me now? After all we've provided for him. He wants me. *Your* wife!" said our child.

"And the problem is?" Mokoena asked nonchalantly.

"I beg your pardon!" Our child placed her hands on her hips.

"What is your problem with that? You give him what he wants. He gives us the business, and life goes on. What's the big deal?" Mokoena feigned ignorance.

"I just cannot believe this! Samson, are you for real?" Our child was bewildered.

"C'mon, Zodwa, don't be uptight here. This is part of doing business."

"I'm your wife, dammit!" Zodwa shouted. "How do you expect me to freely offer my body to another man without a twinge of emotion?"

"Baby love, put your emotions aside. We are running a business here."

"What about my feelings, Samson?" Mokoena's attitude left our child disbelieving. She gaped speechlessly for a few seconds, then blurted out, "That is the most outrageously immoral thing ever said by any husband!" She looked at him as if she had just swallowed a cockroach. We must say that we liked what we saw.

"Morals don't feed an empty stomach, my darling," Mokoena said dismissively.

"Samson, your stomach is barely empty!" Our child looked at Mokoena's round belly with disgust.

"Zodwa, I'm busy here. I am telling you to give this man what he wants, and get it over and done with. I stand to lose lucrative business if..."

"So you've discussed this with him, heh?" our child demanded. Mokoena did not respond. "You rubbish! You discuss me with your business associates like I'm a piece of your property." Our child was now yelling. "You've auctioned me. That's what you've done. Auctioned me like an unwanted piece of furniture!" Veins stood out on her neck as she shouted at him.

"Woman," Mokoena paused to take a deep breath, "we are talking just one night here. One night and we'll get contracts worth hundreds of millions. You either do this or forget about your stake in African Delights. Okay?"

"Okay, fine, I'm resigning. Find someone else to run your rotten company and sleep with your clients. I can't take this any more," said our child, storming out the study. We assisted her in slamming the door behind her.

Mokoena was irritated by the donkey-like stubbornness of a village girl whom he was trying to turn into an asset. Most troubling to him was the amount of business he might lose because of the "unreasonable woman he took as a wife", as he often referred to our child when talking to other people. He thought about the major business opportunities that might slip through his fingers because of our child's unwillingness to dance to his corrupt tune. He started trembling and fighting to catch his breath. He needed his asthma pump. He got up slowly and followed our child to the bedroom.

His pulse rose even further as he found our child throwing clothes into a suitcase. She looked like she was determined to leave.

"Zodwa!" he shouted at our child, struggling to catch his breath. "Where do you think you are going?"

"Out of here!" replied our child. We rejoiced to hear this because our child had always had a place in the waters – if only she listened to the voices of the ancients.

"You are going nowhere!" Mokoena said in between long, dragging breaths. Our child did not respond. She just continued packing.

"Zodwa, I am too rich to be frustrated by stupid things like this!" Our child ignored him, took her suitcases and got ready to go. As she was walking past him, dragging her cases behind her, he tried to obstruct her way.

"You are going nowhere!"

"Get out of my way!" said our child, pushing him with all the power that she could muster. Well, with a little extra power from us. Our responsibility is to protect our creations, and pushing aside obstacles in front of our child was part of protecting her.

The man fell flat on his back with a bang, followed by a momentary earthquake as he bounced like a sumo wrestler. Our child had no idea where she obtained the power to push such a big man. She had forgotten about us. She realised what had happened when she saw a hippopotamus lying still with its eyes closed. At first she thought it was just another act to get her attention, but the manner in which Mokoena had fallen was too convincing. He was clearly unconscious.

Our child got hysterical. She shot out of the house, ran to the cottage at the back of the house and threw her body against Simba's door, banging it with her fists.

"Simba, open up! He is dead. Open up!" Simba, startled by her footsteps, opened the door hastily. She threw herself onto him as soon as he emerged.

"What's wrong?" he asked, gripping her hands, trying

to calm her down.

"He's dead!" she shouted.

"Who?" Simba was confused.

"Samson. He's lying dead in the bedroom."

"What happened?" he asked.

"I didn't do anything to him!" She was incoherent, like a possessed soul.

"Let's go," Simba said and ran towards the house. He did not hesitate before entering the bedroom, as he normally did. He found Mokoena lying on his back. He checked his pulse and found that he was still alive.

"Give me your phone," Simba said to our child.

"Where is it?" she said, fumbling in her handbag. She then rummaged around in the clothes that were spread all over the bed. Simba decided to use the landline to call the ambulance.

"Is he gonna be fine?" our child asked after Simba hung up the phone. "Yes, the ambulance will be here in ten minutes," Simba said, fanning his boss with a towel.

"Oh, my God! What if he dies?"

"He's gonna be fine. Why are your clothes on the bed?" he asked.

"I was –" she hesitated for a moment, "I was packing them. I was getting ready to leave. We had a fight."

"And that's how he collapsed?"

"Oh, Simba, I don't know what I'm gonna do if this man dies."

"No, don't worry, he's not gonna die." We heard the sound of a siren from a distance. "I think that's the ambulance. Open the gate," said Simba. Our child pressed the button and the electric gate opened. The ambulance reversed into the yard. Simba ran out to meet the two paramedics and told them to come to the bedroom. One was lean and of average height, and the other was short and round-bellied. After setting up a drip, the lean one calmly explained, "Looks like he'll be fine. It's probably hypertension. But he'll have to go to hospital immediately."

"Is he diabetic?" the shorter paramedic asked.

"Yes. And asthmatic too," our child explained anxiously.

"He might have to stay in hospital until he is fully recovered," he said as they tried to lift Mokoena. After struggling and failing to get him onto the stretcher, the shorter paramedic asked Simba, "Sir, can you help us to lift him up?"

"Sure, no problem." Our child also helped.

"That's a heavy load!" exclaimed the lean paramedic. There was no comment from the others. "He should regain consciousness soon. But he'll probably have to stay in hospital for a while."

"Okay, we'll follow you to the hospital," Simba said as the two paramedics closed the ambulance doors.

We were there watching when the ambulance drove away.

Our child and Simba hopped into her vehicle. With Simba behind the wheel, they tailed the speeding ambulance, hardly stopping at traffic lights. But the ambulance, blaring its siren and flashing its lights, drove faster and they lost it along the way. They drove to the hospital anyway, where reception referred them to the Intensive Care Unit on the sixteenth floor. As they walked towards the ward, the words ICU in blue lights filled our child with trepidation. They were met at the door by a stocky nurse who introduced herself as Nurse Ramogale. They told her who they were looking for, but when she paged through her file, she could not find Mokoena's name. They explained that he had just been brought in. The nurse led them inside. Our child could not contain her tears when she saw the oxygen mask strapped onto

Mokoena's face. She could not stop blaming herself for what she believed to be his imminent death.

There were other people in the ward visiting other patients. They all spoke in hushed voices. "Look, he's responding very well to treatment," the nurse said.

"But is he gonna make it?" our child asked in between sobs.

"He'll be fine. He was stabilised in the ambulance. His breathing is becoming regular. He is responding very well to atropine. But he's still unconscious at the moment," the nurse explained.

"So, when do you think he'll regain consciousness?" asked Simba.

"Give it a couple of hours. His condition needs close monitoring. The doctor needs to run a few other tests on him."

"More tests?" Simba looked at the nurse with astonishment.

"Yes, Sir. He is both diabetic and asthmatic, isn't he?"

"Yes, he is," Simba and our child responded in unison, the unison that we wished for them.

"That is the reason he needs to be monitored for a while, in case of relapse," the nurse explained.

"That sounds serious," our child remarked.

"His condition is serious, and it will be a while before he is fully recovered. Leave him for now, and maybe come back tomorrow morning," the nurse suggested.

"Do you think he'll be better by then?" our child asked.

"He'll probably have regained consciousness by then," said the nurse. "But avoid saying things that might upset him. As I said, his condition is fragile. It's easy for someone like him to have a relapse."

As soon as they got home, our child helped herself to a glass of red wine. She gulped it down in a single guzzle, and poured a second one. After taking a sip, she called to Simba, who was in the kitchen preparing food, "Would you like some wine?"

"Only after dinner, Mazou," Simba yelled from the kitchen. Our child went to find him with a bottle in one hand and a wine glass in the other. We did not like what we were witnessing. Our child had taken to the bottle, choosing fermented grape instead the pure waters at times of trouble.

"Here, this will boost your appetite," she said, pouring him a glass.

"Are you sure it's just for the appetite?" said Simba, as he took a sip.

"And anything else that matters," our child said, lifting her glass, then stopping as if caught by a spell. "But what if he dies, Simba?" she said pensively.

"He's not gonna die. Why keep saying this?" asked Simba, taking another gulp from his glass.

"Refill?" Our child was waving the bottle before Simba could even respond.

"Yeah. I could do with a little more." He stretched his arm to give his glass to our child. "Tell me, what happened exactly?"

"Simba, that man is evil. Can you believe that he wanted me to sleep with one of the guys from the football federation just because they promised each other some business?" Fresh anger welled up in our child as she remembered the quarrel with her husband.

"What? That's ridiculous! How can he do that?" Simba was furious.

"I'm tired of being a pawn in his game, Simba." Zodwa had tears in her eyes. "He doesn't care about me. All he cares about is money. That man is married to money, Simba. He even told me that ours was a business arrangement from the start, and that sleeping with this guy was just part of doing business. Can you believe that? Isn't he taking me for a fool?" Our child was crying openly now.

"Maybe you should go to bed now. It's way after midnight." Simba abandoned his efforts to cook, thinking it better that Zodwa sleep after drinking so much wine.

Our child ignored this suggestion. "I'm talking to you, Simba. I might not get a chance to say this again," she said, between sobs. "I want you to know how cheaply this man thinks of me."

"We'll talk about this in the morning, Mazou. You must go to bed now."

"So you think I'm a drunk? I am not drunk, Simba. I love my wine, but I know what I am talking about." Our child tried to refill her glass one more time, but the bottle was empty. She put it down, took Simba's glass, and gulped the remaining wine.

"I didn't say that. I can see you are upset. You've had a shock, and it's really late."

"Okay, I'm going to bed. Just need one more drink to help me sleep. Just one," said our child, pointing a finger at the ceiling as she wobbled towards the bar, a part of the house she barely ever visited. "You shouldn't be drinking this much," Simba said.

"What else can I do? Heh, what do you want me to do? Sit here and think about a man who's about to die because of me? Wait for the police to come and take ridiculous statements? I'll be a murder suspect," she said, pointing to her chest. "Are *you* suspicious of me, Simba?"

"No."

"If Samson dies, do you think I'll be responsible for his death?"

"No. You just explained to me what happened."

"But who else would believe my version of the story?

212

Only you, Simba, because you are here with us. You know me. You know him. You know how we live in this house. Everyone else thinks that I am a gold-digger. They don't know the truth," our child said, and started wailing again.

She trailed to the bedroom and threw herself on the bed, with Simba reluctantly following. He took out his handkerchief and held it out to her to wipe her tears, but she continued weeping as if she did not see it. He pulled her close to him, and wiped her tears for her. He kissed her forehead and she dug her face into his chest. Simba tightened the embrace. And soon there was no more crying. It was always intensely intimate when they were in each other's arms.

"I've got to go," said Simba after a while.

"And leave me here alone?" our child asked in a calmer voice.

"Yeah, it's late already, and we have to wake up early tomorrow."

"All the more reason why you should sleep here," she said emphatically.

"I'm feeling guilty about this," Simba said.

"You're feeling guilty? Oh, please. Believe me, you have no reason to."

"It's difficult to do this behind Samson's back. I could barely look him in the eyes after the first time."

"Tell me, Simba, what is the worst form of deception? Lying to yourself about your feelings or keeping the truth from a man who thinks the world revolves around his hand?"

When our child said these words, we thought that she was listening to us. We had been whispering to her, trying to tell her that Simba was the right man for her.

"Deception is deception, I guess."

"So, you would rather deceive yourself? Pretend you

don't care about me when I am what your heart desires? You know that I love you."

"Stop saying that. You'll make me kiss you," Simba said, pulling her against his body. They started kissing. Their clothes began to rain down on the floor. We ran away.

Their lovemaking was a pleasant interlude in our child's frustrating life. It was as if the whole universe belonged to the two of them, a world of joy and happiness. We were victorious, only for a moment. Lying on his chest after a bout of intense lovemaking, our child could not imagine living without Simba. Suddenly it dawned on her that the fairy tale would end as soon as Samson got out of hospital.

"I want him to die," she said out of the blue.

"What?" Simba was shocked.

"I wish he could die. We'll stay here. Sleep in this bed and make love every night." Our child spoke with resolution.

Ours is to protect our creation in the world that we have inhabited before. It is not our responsibility to eliminate, but when our creation speaks, when our creation articulates desires, when our creation needs our protection, we intervene. We listen to our creations and relay their messages to the One Who Appeared First.

"No, no, no, Zodwa. Stop talking like that," Simba objected. "You know we'll be in trouble if anything happens to him. I don't agree."

"I didn't say let's kill him. I just want him to die. That's all."

"Zodwa, you cannot wish a human being away. Especially not your husband. Please stop these kinds of thoughts."

"Don't you wanna be with me?"

"Of course, I want you to be mine. But let's not preempt things. Let life take its natural course."

"Okay, life is gonna take its course then," said our child, kissing Simba on the forehead. "Life is gonna take its course," she murmured, turning to face the opposite direction. She fell asleep while thinking about ways of escaping the matrimonial bondage in which she became entangled at the tender age of twenty-four.

The phone sounded like it was ringing from a distance. Simba opened his eyes and called on our child, but she did not respond. He called again, but to no avail. He tried to shake her awake, but she rolled away from him. Realising that the call could be coming from the hospital, Simba got up to answer the phone.

"Hallo, I'm calling from Quick Med hospital. Is this the Mokoena residence?" Simba recognised the squeaky voice as belonging to the nurse they had met the previous day.

"Yes, it is. Would you like to speak to Mr Mokoena's wife?"

"In fact, you may be the person I want to speak to. Is your name Simba, by any chance?" It sounded more like a rhetorical question than an information-seeking one.

"Yes, it's Simba speaking. Anything wrong?" Anxiety welled up in him.

"I thought I recognised your voice. Mr Mokoena asked me to call you before the end of my shift this morning. He said I should ask you to come here as early as possible."

"Did he say what the matter is?" Simba could not suppress his curiosity. He was impressed to hear that Mokoena was awake and already able to bark orders at people. That was the Mokoena he knew, always in control.

"Well, not exactly. He needs a number of things from the house, though. I think you'll need a pen and paper to write these down."

"Let me get a pen." Simba fumbled in the drawer of the

bedside table and took out a pen. "Yes, I'm ready."

"First of all, you must bring your passport along."

"My passport! What does he want to do with my passport?" Simba asked.

"That was his message, Sir. I didn't ask anything beyond what I was told," the nurse said, leaving no room for further debate.

"Okay, sorry about that. What else?"

"His safe in the study."

"A safe in the study?" Simba said in puzzlement. He never heard of that one before. "Yes, Sir," the nurse said confidently. "He said you'll have to remove the books on the shelf above his desk, and you'll see the space for the safe."

"Fine. I will look for it," Simba said, waiting for the next instruction.

"Can you do that now, Sir?" the nurse asked.

"You want me to do that now? Please hold on, then." He placed the handset on the table and went to Mokoena's study. He removed the books from the shelf and found a small handle, which he twisted. It revealed a pigeonhole in which he found a small and compact safe. He returned to the bedroom and picked up the handset.

"Okay, I've got it," he announced.

"Good, the last thing he's asked for is his laptop," said the nurse.

"Is he fine to use a laptop?" Simba was concerned about Mokoena rushing to do work while his condition was still fragile.

"Sir, that's what I have been instructed to say. Mr Mokoena wants his laptop brought to the hospital," the nurse said emphatically.

"So it's the laptop, the safe and my passport?" Simba checked the details.

"That's correct, Sir," the nurse assured him as she ended

the call.

"Is Samson fine?" our child asked. She was now fully awake and worried.

"I think so," Simba said, still a bit confused.

"What do you mean, you think so? What were you talking about?"

"The nurse says I must bring my passport to the hospital. Mokoena told her to call me before the end of her shift. That's why she called so early." He was apprehensive.

"Oh no, he's not doing that again," said our child, annoyance written across her face.

"What? What do you think he's doing?" Simba said, overwhelmed with curiosity.

"Changing the will."

"Changing the will?" Simba was still lost.

"Yes. That's what he does every time he fights with someone close to him. The last time I checked, I was his beneficiary. Now that we've had a misunderstanding, he probably wants to make you his beneficiary. Hence you have to take your passport."

"I see." Our child's words were beginning to sink in. Simba concluded that she knew how to handle this matter better than he did. "So what should I do?"

"What else can you do? Just do as he says. Don't do anything that might upset him. Otherwise you'll be blamed for his death."

"Stop saying that!" Simba exclaimed.

"What?" Our child feigned innocence.

"The 'D' word."

"You mean *Death*?" Zodwa said, smiling.

"Yes, that."

"Okay, Samson's days in this world are numbered, and you don't wanna be the vehicle for his exit..." our child quipped sarcastically.

"Enough already! This is no joke! I've got to go." Simba jumped into the *en suite* bathroom, noticing that the shower was particularly vast to cater for Mokoena's bulk. After showering, he wrapped a towel around his waist and looked at his half-naked body in the mirror. The mirror was misty due to the vapour, and he couldn't see his face clearly. He was disappointed. He wanted to see what a prospective millionaire looked like.

Simba put on a pair of jeans, a white T-shirt and a leather jacket before kissing our child goodbye. He drove off in Mokoena's giant car, the black Chrysler C300. At the hospital, he was surprised to find Nurse Ramogale, the same nurse who had attended to them the previous night. She had bags below her eyes, a clear sign that she had not slept.

Nurse Ramogale led Simba to a side ward, where Mokoena had been relocated to a private room. Mokoena was conversing with a young man. By the look of things, his condition had improved. The oxygen mask was hanging on the drip stand next to his bed. He still had a drip inserted into the back of his left hand, and the strong urine filling the catheter bag next to the bed was a disgusting orange colour, but the young man did not seem to mind the sight.

We were there, watching.

We had lent a hand in shoving Mokoena. We did not want him to die – we do not eliminate. That is the responsibility of the One Who Appeared First. We were glad that Mokoena had survived.

We saw the young man taking Mokoena through some documents. The young man wore a black suit, a white shirt and a red tie. He had glasses that gave him an intellectual aura. Simba watched Mokoena as he squinted, trying to read the fine print on the thick documents. He concluded that our child might be right. The young man was probably

Mokoena's lawyer! He cleared his throat as a way of drawing their attention.

"Hey, Simba, you are just on time," Mokoena said enthusiastically, welcoming Simba to his new office. "Come and meet my lawyer, Clarence September," he said, pointing at the young man. Simba grinned and stretched his arm to greet him.

"Nice meeting you, Sir," said Simba, shaking hands with Clarence.

"Likewise," Clarence responded.

"Let me attend to my beautiful nurse first." Mokoena reached for his safe, shielding the keypad from them with his body as he punched in the numbers of his code. Simba and Clarence both looked away politely.

"Okay, there you go, my darling," said Mokoena, handing over a stack of R200 notes to the nurse.

"Thank you, Sir," she said, beaming. "I really appreciate this."

"That's what you get when you treat Samson Mokoena well!"

"By all means, Sir. Please feel free to call me on my mobile if there's anything else you want," she said as she left, all smiles.

"What was that for?" Simba whispered.

"They had to remove some pauper so I could get this private room. Otherwise I'd be lying in the open wards watching people dying every minute." While Mokoena maintained that one should always soothe the hands of one's handlers, Simba never thought that the soothing of hands applied even in hospitals. The man would bribe his way into heaven if possible.

"So this is your new beneficiary?" asked Clarence, bringing them back to the issue at hand.

"A beneficiary?" Simba echoed, faking amazement.

"Let me explain the reason I called you here," Mokoena intervened. His breathing was still hoarse and noisy. "I am signing my will and, as you know, other than Zodwa, you are the closest person to me. After I came back from exile, I vowed not to have anything to do with those lousy whiners who call themselves my relatives. Only you, Simba, know my life struggle." He paused every few words to breathe. "That is why I want you to be my beneficiary."

"How can I be your beneficiary when your wife is still alive, Sir?" Simba tried to display some resistance.

"Simba, don't start that nonsense now. I say you are going to be my beneficiary. Understand?" Mokoena's lower lip began to tremble as it always did when he got angry.

"With all due respect, Sir. I just cannot find it in my heart to accept such an arrangement while your wife is still here. It's only logical that…"

"Why, because Zodwa told you not to accept it?" said Mokoena angrily.

"No, Sir. The thing is…"

"Listen here, Simba," Mokoena interjected. "I know some people think I'm a fool and you may be starting to believe that. Let me tell you now, I am no fool, my boy, and I'll never be one." He stopped to inhale oxygen.

"I know you are no such thing, Sir." Simba wanted to withdraw, but even silence might now be viewed as a sign of defiance.

"You think I'm a fool too, Simba. You've been fucking my wife and you think I don't know that." Simba's eyes rolled around the ward as Mokoena jumped to a point he did not anticipate. Clarence fixed his gaze on the floor, carefully avoiding eye contact with either of them.

"But you know what, Simba, I like it. I know how far my trust can go with you." Mokoena paused for another breath. "You are not like other unpredictable fools. You've stayed with me for almost four years now, and you've never tried to take advantage of me. The only thing you can't resist is the same thing that has overpowered humankind since time immemorial." He took a sip from a glass of water on the tray next to his bed. "Who are you to resist? And I know my wife is fine, that's why you couldn't wait to get into her pants," he chuckled.

Simba looked at him blankly. He did not know whether to laugh, smile or frown. He took a quick glance at Clarence, and their eyes met. The lawyer looked equally scared.

"What if I decide to tap yours, as you have been doing to my wife?" Mokoena said.

This was too much for Clarence. "Can I leave you two and you can call me when you are ready to go through the papers?" he tried to excuse himself.

"You are going nowhere," Mokoena stated emphatically. "What kind of a lawyer are you?"

"I just thought…"

"Don't tell me about your thoughts here! Your job is to process the legal papers. Simba, I called you to come and sign my policy documents as the beneficiary. I've already put you in my will. Now I'm giving you two options in the presence of a legal representative. Either you agree to this, or I do to you what you've been doing to my wife. Which one do you choose?" He coughed out the last words.

"I'll sign, Sir," Simba promptly relented.

"You'll sign?"

"Yes, Sir. I'll sign."

"Okay! Now, let's do some business. Clarence, give him the papers." He adjusted his bed to an almost upright position. Clarence gave the documents to Simba. He scribbled his signature and gave them back to Samson.

"That wasn't so difficult, was it?" Mokoena said with a triumphant smile.

"No, Sir. I was just worried that it would seem like I wanted to inherit your wealth when you die. You know, people are killed for their funeral policies these days."

"Stop dreaming, Simba. You think I'm about to die? Never. I'm going nowhere. I'll live long enough to see you off to your Shona ancestors. I'll shed a tear or two when I hear about your departure, and drive slowly behind the hearse carrying your coffin. And after burying you, I'll piss on your grave." He laughed at his own joke. Simba did not find it funny. Clarence chuckled a bit, no doubt to please his client.

"One last thing, Simba. Tell Zodwa not to bother coming here unless she has done what she's got to do."

"What has she got to do, Sir?" Simba wondered.

"She knows exactly what I'm talking about. I'm sure you know it, too."

"I don't know anything, Sir. But I will tell her."

"As a warning to you: if she doesn't do what she is expected to do, you might have to take her place. After all, you have already taken my place in her."

Simba wandered around the hospital, devastated. He had heard about the sexual transformation that took place among men in the prison cells, and had always been terrified of finding himself there. Now he was faced with a similar situation, without even having been imprisoned.

We, the Down People, are the inhabitants of both worlds. We lift our creations on our shoulders to reach the highest skies, while we remain rooted in the waters.

That evening, our child heard Simba calling her from the kitchen. She emerged from the bedroom wearing a black knee-length silk gown, eager to embrace him.

"Mazou, I think you have to do it," he said.

"What?" our child was caught unawares.

"Do it. It's just one night." Our child could see in his eyes that what his mouth was saying remained contrary to what the heart was feeling.

"I cannot believe this! Simba, is this you? Is this you, telling me to sleep with another man? What is wrong with men in this world?" Zodwa threw her hands in the air.

"You'd better do it and get it done with, once and for all," Simba said, hardening his heart.

"If it's easy for you men to sleep with someone you don't have feelings for, it's not that easy for us women. Sex is not just a physical act," our child shouted.

"But you've subjected other young girls to the same situation." Simba did not fear being confrontational, after having been threatened with what he believed was sodomy.

"Simba, whose side are you on, heh? Am I missing something here? I just cannot believe my ears. I took you into my confidence! You know very well how African Delights was established!" She turned to leave.

"Okay, I'm sorry. It's just ... please don't go." He took her by the arm as she tried to shove past him. "Mazou, please listen to me."

Our child fixed her gaze on his eyes with her arms akimbo. "Okay, I'm all ears." "This is a very complex situation. A lot is at stake here," he implored.

"What's at stake? Is Samson gonna remove you from the will as his beneficiary?"

"No, it's not that. He knows about us. He knows we've been having an affair," he explained.

"How did he get to know about that?" Our child was astonished.

"I don't know. He just knows," said Simba, shrugging his shoulders in despair.

"And you admitted to it?"

Simba nodded.

"Stupid!"

"What do you mean? I couldn't deny it when it was clear that he knew."

"He's been suspicious for a very long time, but he does not have any tangible proof. You know, the phone call this morning was a trap," she concluded.

"What do you mean, it was a trap?" Simba was still confused.

"He knew you wouldn't answer the landline before six in the morning unless you had slept in the house." Our child solved the puzzle for Simba because we gave her foresight. We wished she had listened to us before.

"Damn! You're right." It began to dawn on him how easy it had been for Mokoena to set them up.

"We could've denied it, but now you've messed it all up. And you expect me to clean up by selling my soul?"

"That man is threatening to screw me!" Simba dropped his bombshell.

"What?" Our child was astounded.

"Yeah. He wants to do it to me."

"So it's true," said our child thoughtfully.

"What's true?" Simba felt ignorant.

"I've heard rumours that he's been sleeping with his caddies in hotels when he goes away for golf tournaments."

"But you can't prove that."

"Yeah, I can't prove it now. But this piece of information would be good ammunition."

"What do you mean?"

"I want a divorce. This could be our breakthrough."

"But he can still deny it."

"That's why you have to sleep with him. Then we'll have tangible evidence."

"What, me sleep with another man? Are you out of

your mind?" Simba felt insulted.

"He might even settle out of court. Then we'll have our fair share of his wealth, and we can marry," reasoned our child.

"Don't even go that far. I'll never sleep with another man. Over my dead body," Simba said.

"He doesn't have to penetrate you. Just a gesture that's sexually suggestive, that will be good enough to press charges. Please, Simba, you've got to work with me on this."

"Mazou, please understand. What you are asking me to do is totally unnatural."

"And it's natural for me to sleep with an old German man I find repulsive? Simba, it is you that I want. I will sleep with you any time and anywhere in the world. But I just can't take my clothes off for a man I don't have feelings for." Our child seemed helpless as she spoke.

"Mazou, please do this for me. For us. You just have to do it once, and all will be well. I just can't have another man touching my skin. It's evil," he pleaded.

"I don't know, Simba," she said slowly. "I really don't like this. Why must I be the one to compromise all the time?"

Simba could smell victory. "If there is anyone who is compromised here, it's me, my love. I just can't imagine you with another man. I want you to be my wife, Mazou," he said, pulling her to his chest. He wrapped his strong arms around her body. We liked what we saw.

"Simba, are you serious about this?"

"It's torture to me, Mazou. But it's something that we have to go through," he said.

"If there is anything that I want in my life, it's to be with you as my husband," our child said, and burst into tears. He held her tightly against his chest. "I want you as my husband, Simba," she said sobbing. "I know you'll make me happy."

"I'll be the happiest man alive, Mazou. Let's just get over this hurdle."

"But won't this bring a cloud that will always hang over our relationship?"

"It won't," he assured her, "take my word for it. I love you too much to judge you for this. This is about our survival. You are doing this for us."

Our child turned to give him her back. She kept quiet and stared into space. After a while she said, "I wanna be alone tonight."

"Are you sure?" Simba said hesitantly.

"Yeah, I've got to think about this." Simba was somewhat relieved to hear this.

"Okay, if you say so, it's fine," he said getting up. "But don't hesitate to call when you need me, okay?" he said as he left the room. He was relieved that she was wavering. He was confident she loved him too much to refuse his request.

After many tears, our child got up and went into her bathroom. In the mirror, her eyes were swollen. She washed her face in cold water, then put on her night-robe and sat on the bed, still staring into nothingness. After a while she reached for her BlackBerry and started writing a text message. It read: *"Dear Mr Schweinesteiger, you'll get the best of African delights, at the best price."*

We overwhelmed her with emotion and her whole body began to tremble uncontrollably. She thought a drink would help, not realising that we were trying to send a message to her. She went to the bar and took a bottle of red wine, but she couldn't find the corkscrew. She called Simba on the intercom. Within a minute, he was in the house.

"What's wrong, Mazou?" he asked in exasperation.

"I want the corkscrew."

"We were in the bedroom the last time we used it. Let's

look for it there." He first looked on the bedroom floor. Satisfied that it was not lying there, he lifted the bed. "Check underneath," he advised.

"There it is," said our child, kneeling to look under the bed.

"So, will you join me?" she asked.

"Sure, why not?" he said, taking the bottle from her and opening it. "What were you doing up at this hour, anyway?"

"What time is it?" She had lost track of the hours.

"It's midnight and you are about to open a bottle of wine," he said, trying to make her remorseful. "And you might have to travel to Mpumalanga tomorrow."

"You don't know what I'm going through, Simba," she said, shaking her head. "I've been thinking about what we discussed."

Our child looked around for her mobile phone, took it and held it to Simba's face.

"Look, this is what I've written."

"And you haven't sent it?" Simba asked after reading the message.

"I just can't get myself to send it," she said.

"C'mon, Mazou. Remember you have to make travel arrangements to meet these guys at the Kruger. There aren't many flights to that small airport."

"Travel arrangements are the least of my worries. I've been staring at that message for hours on end," she said, helping herself to another glass of wine.

"Okay, let me send it for you."

"Whatever," said our child dismissively. Simba pressed the green button without hesitation and the message was gone. We watched in amazement as our choice of compassion for our child sent the message to Schweinesteiger. Much as we liked Simba, we were not in control of his actions. He had his own Down People to look after him. Sadly, we are not responsible for the changes that human beings undergo, much as we are not responsible of the changes in weather.

"Done!" said Simba triumphantly.

The phone beeped only a minute later. "That's his response. Please read it because I don't wanna see what he's written," said our child wretchedly. Simba opened the message and read it to her:

"How much are we talking here?"

Simba looked at our child with a glimmer of excitement. "You see, he's willing to pay anything. Let's say a hundred thousand and see what he says!"

"I don't give a damn, okay!" our child replied, shuddering with revulsion. Simba tapped in the figure of R100 000 and sent the message. Two minutes passed without a response. Simba kept looking at the phone, but no message was forthcoming. Time slowed right down. They finished the bottle of wine, and Simba opened another one, trying to keep Zodwa happy. He was on tenterhooks, and even considered sending another text saying that the previous message was only a joke, and they would be prepared to settle for a lower price. After nearly two hours, when they were halfway through the second bottle, when they had almost forgotten what had brought them to that bedroom in the first place, they heard a beep coming from our child's phone. Simba jumped to the phone and read the message. "My goodness!" he exclaimed with glee.

"What? What's that?" Our child tried to take the phone from Simba's hand.

"He did it!"

"He did what?" our child asked, perplexed by Simba's delight.

"Baby, we are rich. He deposited the whole R100 000 into your account. Look!" He showed her the message.

Baer Schweinesteiger had deposited the money via internet banking. "Now I wish I had asked for more!"

"Oh, please," said our child irritably.

"Let's do your bookings. Where's your laptop?"

"Just make sure you don't book me the red-eye flight."

"Red-eye flight. What's that?" he wondered.

"The early-morning flight. Passengers on those flights usually have red eyes because of lack of sleep," she explained.

"They don't have one of those to Mpumalanga. The first available flight is at nine o'clock in the morning," he said, staring at the computer screen.

Simba processed the booking for our child. They woke up very early the next morning and drove to the airport, where Zodwa got on the flight.

Our child had been to Kruger Park numerous times before in the course of business. She didn't understand why tourists would want to go through the torture of leaving their chalets at four in the morning in order to spot a lion. In fact, she had never seen all of the over-rated Big Five in a single day. In all her visits, she had seen lions only on two occasions. These are the thoughts we whispered into our child's ear as she travelled with a bunch of European tourists who had come to South Africa under the pretext of teaching Africa how to host an event as spectacular as the football tournament.

They were now gathered on top of a hill to watch the sunset. Our child was a passive participant. She found no joy in watching the setting of the sun. She had seen the sunset almost every day of her life. She got no pleasure from watching nature taking its course, day in and day out. But the tourists clicked their cameras with glee, trying to capture pictures of every second of the sunset. As the sun slowly descended behind the mountains, our child began to think about what brought her to the nature reserve. That she was about to allow a strange man to touch her was disgusting.

When a drop of rain falls from the sky, it cannot return.

As the night fell, the sky lit up with a galaxy of stars and the moon smiled from a distance. It had been a beautiful day, and the night was proving to be quite a strong contender. It was the kind of night that Chinua Achebe would describe as capable of making even a cripple hungry for a walk. The whole delegation sat outside, admiring the stars.

Europeans are really strange people, our child thought. They come all the way from their cold countries just to stare at things in Africa. They are never part of the action. No music, no dance, no *braai*. Just staring. Staring at people. Staring at animals. Staring at birds. Staring at plants. And even staring at space. That's how they enjoy Africa. Just staring.

She twitched and felt an itchy area with her hand. There was a small lump, and she knew that she had been bitten by a mosquito. We whispered to our child that it was time to leave. She had been around strangers long enough, wearing a constant smile as she was introduced to members of the delegation. She excused herself with the hope of spending a bit of time alone in the chalet.

"Are you sure?" asked Schweinesteiger.

"Yes, I tend to react badly to mosquito bites," she explained.

"Okay, I'll join you later then," Schweinesteiger said.

Barely an hour later she heard the screech of the door, and footsteps stumbling to the bathroom. The man's urine trickled slowly into the toilet bowl, like a leaking roof after heavy rains. It must have been the longest piss she had ever heard. He farted at least ten times while urinating. After what seemed like an eternity, he flushed the toilet.

She heard him wash his hands and close the bathroom door behind him.

Our child looked at him with disgust as he approached the bed. The man was rich, but he wore threadbare khaki trousers that could pass for a servant's uniform. He sat on the bed and took off his clothes. When he tried to open the blanket, we assisted our child in holding it tight, our last-ditch attempt to protect our child.

"Take a shower before coming to bed. You've been sweating all day," our child said confrontationally.

"You want me to take a shower? It's okay. I will." He got up and staggered towards the bathroom. It must have been the quickest shower in history. Within minutes, the man was back with his stringy wet hair, ready to join her in bed.

"Please dry your hair. You'll give me a cold." He looked at her, smiled and shook his head, making it clear he recognised her delaying tactics. She watched the man bending over and pointing the hairdryer at his head. Our child wished the dryer was a loaded rifle. She imagined his brain splattered all over the floor. We were not averse to her wishes, but these are the decisions of the One Who Appeared First.

Once he had dried his hair, he took off his robe and exposed his naked body to our child. She knew the time had come. She did not want to kiss him. She removed her underwear and spread her beautiful brown body across the white linen sheets. Baer Schweinesteiger was about to penetrate her and reach her depths, fulfilling what remained fantasy to many young men. We could not run away. We wanted to be there for our child. We wanted to make the experience miserable for both of them.

Our child could barely feel him inside her, but his pulse rate had increased. As he clung to her tightly, he told her to chirp like a monkey.

"What?" She thought her ears were playing some trick on her.

"Chirp like a monkey!" he repeated.

"That's crazy!" she retorted.

"Chirp like a monkey!" he yelled.

"You are mad!"

"Chirp like a monkey, chirp like a monkey, chirp like a monkey!"

"Why?" Our child was totally confused.

"I'm in Africa. Chirp like a monkey. It's an adventure. I want to feel Africa."

Indeed, earlier that day our child had felt like a monkey in a cage as several members of the football federation's contingent had taken turns to look at her like a captured animal of an endangered species. They were there to visit primitive Africa, and to them, women formed part of the tourism landscape in the Dark Continent. They neither had minds nor feelings of their own. What mattered was the landscape hidden between their thighs.

"Chirp like a monkey!"

"Grweeeeh, grweeeeh, grweeeeeeh…" Our child made the sound out of annoyance. She realised that the man would not stop until she co-operated.

"Chirp like a monkey!"

"Grweeeeh, grweeeeh, grweeeeeeh…" She was not sure about her version of a monkey sound, but she wanted the whole thing to be over with. It seemed to work because the man exclaimed, "Uhahahahah…!" and then collapsed on top of her. She pushed him off her and he rolled to the other side of the bed. A few minutes later, he started snoring loudly.

Our child felt the horrid crawl of fear after sleeping with Mr Schweinesteiger, something that had never been there after she had first slept with Simba, or after their subsequent trysts. She did not think about her husband, but she felt she had betrayed Simba. She got up and went to the bathroom. The man had used a condom, but she wanted to cleanse away every bit of fluid that came as a result of their intercourse. Yes, intercourse is what they had. There was no love-making. Satisfied that there was not a drop of the man's semen in her body, she decided to take a long shower. She scrubbed her body vigorously, hoping to rid herself of every bit of sweat, his smell, anything that could remind her of what had just happened.

After half an hour, Baer Schweinesteiger walked to the bathroom, stark naked, and found our child rinsing her body. He looked at her with a sense of accomplishment, spanked her buttocks, and murmured, "That was delightful." She felt like vomiting at the sight of his naked body. The man had freckles all over his back, including his wrinkled backside.

She wiped her body dry and put on a gown. She went to the bedroom, but instead of getting under the blankets, she took a pillow and the spare blanket from the wardrobe.

"And where are you taking those?" Schweinesteiger asked as our child went past him, headed for the lounge. "I'm gonna watch TV," she responded without looking at him.

"At this time?"

"Yes, at this time."

"Look, Zodwa. I've been inside you and you cannot do anything to change that, okay?" Our child felt like telling him that she had barely felt him inside her, but decided to ignore him. Surely he was satisfied with his feeble effort.

"Just come to bed," he said.

Our child switched the TV on and fixed her eyes on the screen, suppressing the urge to respond to Schweinesteiger's provocation.

"Okay, I'll leave you alone, I'll leave you alone," he said as he walked back to the bedroom. The next thing our child heard were uproarious snores coming from the bedroom. She turned up the volume of the TV, hoping to drown the irritating sound, but it continued to bother her. She put the pillow over her ear and covered herself with the blanket.

Our child heard the familiar sound of *Weekend Live's* theme song. Her heart wanted to jump out of her mouth when she saw the picture of Baer Schweinesteiger. It was not the first time she had seen Schweinesteiger on TV, but today was different. The word "SUSPENDED" ran across his face. Our child sat upright and paid attention. The newsreader announced that the federation had suspended Schweinesteiger, pending investigation of corruption allegations. He was suspected of having embezzled over two hundred million euros. The case was to be heard shortly after the World Cup tournament.

"What?" our child exclaimed. Tears streamed out of her eyes in torrents. She went to the bedroom and collected her clothes, still crying, while the man snored the morning away.

Her phone rang and she saw that it was Simba calling. She was not in the mood for a chat, and answered the phone without much enthusiasm.

"Hey, did you hear?" Simba asked.

"Did I hear what?" She assumed he had heard about Schweinesteiger's suspension.

"So, they didn't call you. Mr Mokoena has suffered a heart attack. I'm told to come to the hospital urgently."

Zodwa was shocked. "How come no one said anything about it to me?" she asked.

"They must have forgotten. I'm on my way there. Please get here as soon as possible."

She felt that Simba was now in charge of her life. "Okay, I'll be there in about three hours. I'm on my way to the airport right now."

"Please try to rush, because it sounded urgent," Simba said, ending the call. He took the keys, looked around the house, gently nodded to himself, locked the door with a broad smile and went towards the giant vehicle.

When Simba got to the hospital he was met by the same Nurse Ramogale who had received them on the first night that Mokoena was admitted. She asked him to sit down.

"Mr Mokoena left us about an hour ago," she said in a low dignified voice. He did not know where her squeakiness had gone.

"What do you mean, he left you?" Simba asked, not understanding.

"Sir, Mr Mokoena is no more."

"What?" Simba grabbed the armrest of the chair he was sitting on. He got up and then sat down again. All along the nurse sat calmly in the chair behind the desk.

"He suffered a heart attack at about seven this morning," she explained.

"A heart attack?" Simba could not make sense of the situation.

"Yes, it happened while he was watching the news."

"I can't believe this." His mouth was agape with shock.

"Since you are his next-of-kin, you'll have to sign all the official documents and take his death certificate. You'll have to wait a few hours, though."

"Okay, I'll wait."

He went to find a bench and sat cupping his face with both his hands and staring at the floor. He took regular glances at his wristwatch, wondering when our child would arrive.

We are the voices of the ancients.

We have been here before, we are here now, and we have foresight for the future. Our child arrived at the hospital and went straight up to ICU on the sixteenth floor, hoping to give Mokoena and Simba a piece of her mind. Her sharp heels made staccato-like sounds as she walked fast along the tiled hospital corridors. She found Simba with two female nurses, busy signing documents in the small office at the entrance to the ward. They were so engrossed in what they were doing that our child decided to ignore them and go straight to Mokoena's side ward.

When she got to the bed, she found it empty and tidy. She went back to the office. She stood for a few seconds, hoping to get their attention. The nurses were talking and laughing out loud with Simba as he continued signing documents. One nurse turned to look in her direction, but joined in the chat again without attending to her.

Zodwa lost her temper. She wanted to see her sick husband and she was tired of waiting. They all turned and stared in shock as she stormed into the office.

"Mazou," said Simba with astonishment, "you are here already."

"Yes, I'm here! Now where is Samson?" Simba exchanged glances with the two nurses and dropped his eyes momentarily. He then lifted his head and addressed our child: "Hey, Mazou, something, heh, something strange happened here today," he stuttered.

"What, what happened? What does that have to do with Samson's whereabouts anyway?" Clearly she was not getting the message.

"He had a heart attack," Simba stated.

"You told me about that already," our child said, still baffled.

"He didn't make it this time," Simba explained.

"What? He's dead?" she asked, devastated.

"Yeah, I was shocked too. But what can we say, he's been ill for quite some time now. At least he's released from all the suffering."

"You mean it's good that he's dead?"

"No, that's not what I meant. What I'm saying is, eh, because his health has been quite delicate, we shouldn't be surprised that this has happened."

"Simba, my husband has just died, and all you are telling me is that I must not worry because he was sick anyway?"

"Oh, so you two were married?" the stocky nurse said, with puzzlement on her face.

"Yes, we were married. Tell me, how did this happen? According to your last reports, he was doing fine! We were told that his condition had stabilised, and he was here only to finish the course of treatment."

"He was doing well, Ma'am, that's true. But the heart attack was sudden. It happened while he was watching the seven-o'-clock news this morning. Unfortunately it was sudden and severe, and as a result, we couldn't resuscitate him," the nurse explained sympathetically.

"You said it happened while watching the news on *Weekend Live*?"

"Yes, we believe so, Ma'am."

"Damn it! I should have known," she said, as the realisation dawned.

"Can I have a moment alone with Mrs Mokoena, please?" asked Simba, and the nurses left the office reluctantly. As soon as they were alone, Simba asked: "What was on the news?"

"Schweinesteiger."

"Which Schweinesteiger?"

"The one you made me sleep with."

"So you did it?"

"As if I had a choice. It turns out he no longer has any decision-making influence. He's been suspended from the federation."

"What?"

"Yeah, it was in the news on *Weekend Live* this morning."

"So, all the business deals that Samson was due to get will fall through?"

"Business deals!" Our child took a step back and stared at Simba with disgust. "Business deals are all you care about? You don't care about what I had to go through because of you!" The nurses had crept back to listen to the two lovers fighting.

"Mazou, please don't shout," Simba cautioned, as he noticed that they had gathered an audience.

"You can't tell me how to speak. You are the one who told me to sleep with that man. Now all you care about is the wealth that you stand to inherit out of the unscrupulous deals that Samson made. What is the difference between you and Samson, then? Tell me!"

"I've got to go," Simba said, and he turned and left. Our child was dumbstruck.

The nurses pretended to be busy as Simba walked through the passage. Armed with a file under his arm, keys and a mobile phone in his hand, he walked through what seemed like a guard of honour formed by the hospital staff and visitors. The crowd made way for Simba like the Red Sea opening for the Israelites.

As everyone was still looking at Simba with astonishment, they did not notice that our child was heading in the opposite direction. At the end of that corridor on the sixteenth floor was a big window, big enough for a man to walk through. Our child hurried towards it, opened it, and jumped. We were watching as our best creation flew towards us.

We are the Down People. When a drop of rain falls from the sky, we do not turn it away, instead, we open our hands and welcome it back into the waters.

Afterword: Ten Years of Writing

◆

I PUBLISHED MY FIRST two short stories in 2001. They were published in a Rhodes University journal called *Aerial*. It was a typical low-budget publication – spiral bound and poorly designed. But with all its imperfections, this is the publication that gave me courage and catapulted me into the heights that I have reached in my writing so far.

Since that first publication in *Aerial*, I have appeared in various anthologies, journals, newspapers and magazines all over the world. Excited by my successful publication in 2001, I was foolish enough to resign from my job in Grahamstown and pursue further literary studies at Wits University in Johannesburg. It was here that fellow creative writers gave me flattering feedback, alleging that my story "Mpumi's Assignment" reminded them of Can Themba's short story "The Suit". I revisited "The Suit", and after reading it several times, I started asking questions about what happened to the man who escaped half-naked out the window. This was the birth of "The Suit Continued".

"The Suit Continued" is by far my most celebrated short story to date. It has been published about six times, both in South Africa and abroad. In March 2007, I met a new novelist, Zukiswa Wanner, soon to become a force to be reckoned with on the literary scene. After reading "The Suit Continued", Wanner decided to present a woman's perspective of events in the suit stories, which she titled "The Dress That Fed the Suit". Not to be outdone, I followed up with another story, "The Lost Suit". These three stories form Part One of this book, and are a tribute to Can Themba, described by Lewis Nkosi as "the supreme intellectual *tsotsi* of them all".

Having grown up in Joza Township, Grahamstown, during the emergency years of the 1980s, I have vivid memories of occasional encounters with white people. Since I believe that the past has bearing in shaping the present, I had to combine memory and imagination in crafting childhood stories. The stories "White Encounters" and "Bhontsi's Toe" are drawn from experiences of interactions with white people in various circumstances. The last story in Part Two, "Hunger", is set in the mid-1990s, and explores race relations after the jettisoning of apartheid. In a sense, this story forms a connection between the old and the new socio-political orders in South Africa.

In 2009, a group of ladies invited me to what was supposed to be a book club discussion at Maponya Mall in Soweto, Johannesburg. Only three ladies of that so-called book club showed up that Saturday morning. It turned out that they were not so much interested in discussing my first novel, *When a Man Cries*, as finding out the truth about my characters. In particular, they were determined to discover whether I was Themba, the protagonist of the novel. After a two-hour interrogation, I drove back to Pretoria and wrote the story "The Truth", introducing new twists into the tale. I started the story with the phrase, "Truth is forever elusive". Almost a year after having written this piece, I came across Harold Pinter's Nobel Prize acceptance speech, where he uses the phrase, "Truth in drama is forever elusive". At this time, I had already written "The Other Truth" and "So Many Truths" to complete the trilogy of the Truth stories, which form Part Three of this collection.

Sometime in 2009, after reading the synopsis of the then soon-to-be-launched Zakes Mda's novel, *Black Diamond*, I wrote to the man accusing him of getting a head start in writing *my* story. At the time, I had started what I was hoping would become my next book, exploring the lifestyle of the new black elite and the influence of wealth and power in contemporary society. The lead character would have been a former beauty queen, now plying her trade as an escort agent. However, as I pointed out in my note to Mda, my escort agent was "high class" compared to his. It was to take another year before I could finish the three stories that make up Part Four.

The short stories in this publication are a celebration of ten years of active contribution to the literary landscape. They are also a celebration of love. In 2001 I met and fell in love with a woman who was later to become my wife and the mother of our two daughters. Miliswa also became the first victim of my writing ambitions, as she had to bear the brunt of reading even my most senseless first drafts. I know she was not always keen to do so, but I am grateful that she took time to read and give me critical feedback. I cannot forget our two daughters, my self-appointed editorial assistants, Mihlali and Qhama, without whom I would have finished this book two years ago!

In the past ten years, the majority of which I have spent living a nomadic life, I met many wonderful people who have influenced me. Through my job as an official in the Department of Arts and Culture (DAC), and my involvement in literary circles as an enthusiast, I was able to meet and befriend some great minds, all of whom inspired me in my creative output. They know who they are, but due to space limitations, I cannot name all of them here. However, it is a well-known secret that my adopted son, brother and mentor, Thando Mgqolozana, took the position of second reviewer and editor after my wife. Once I passed this stage, I usually gathered enough courage to give my scripts to the writers' writer, Zukiswa Wanner, and then to other friends and colleagues.

My writing has always been an attempt at recreating reality – combining lived experience and imagined worlds. The stories in this publication are, therefore, a product of a collective genius of people who have touched my life in a variety of ways. They cover several decades, beginning in Sophiatown of the 1950s. I am fortunate to have met fathers, friends and colleagues who were part of the Sophiatown generation. I am indebted to *tata* Don Mattera, a *toppie* who taught me not to be a *moegoe*, for his compassion, invaluable wisdom and willingness to share anecdotes about Sophiatown. The brutal honesty of South Africa's National Poet Laureate, Keorapetse Kgositsile, once described by Mbulelo Mzamane as a "very short man who is never short of words", gave me strength and determination to keep trying. Most of all, he taught me not to take myself, but my work seriously. I thank him for the gifts of love, life and laughter!

I am indebted to all the readers and reading promotion entities (book clubs, literary festivals, book fairs and the media) that kept reminding me that I was once a writer. The ReadSA family, with whom I criss-crossed the country promoting reading, brings out the best in me. I thank the DAC Book Club, especially the incumbent chairperson, Sibongile Nxumalo, for their continued support and determination to make reading popular in our society.

Lastly, I would not have been able to share these stories with you if not for my publisher, Jacana Media, who thought my hallucinations were worth publishing. On the same note, I cannot think of a more suitable editor than Helen Moffett, who brought this baby to life. Now that you have read this book, you have unwittingly embarked on a journey retracing my literary trajectory of the past decade. I trust that this tiny drop into the sea of world literature will create ripples that will reverberate beyond my immediate surroundings and make a difference to humanity.

Other Jacana Literary Foundation Titles

Planet Savage
Tuelo Gabonewe

Hear Me Alone
Thando Mgqolozana

*The Zombie
and the Moon*
Peter Merrington